Courting! Where had that thought come from?

Thomas wasn't going to be doing any courting. Dropping the nutcracker, he shoved his chair back from the table.

Emma and Cilla looked over in surprise at the ensuing screech against the linoleum. Thomas pushed to his feet. "Bag's empty. Time we went home."

Brushing walnut shell fragments from her apron, Emma rose from the table as well. "*Denki* for all the help. I can't believe we've finished that much already."

"Can we do it again sometime?" Cilla asked as she chose a nut from her bowl and nibbled on it.

Emma glanced at Thomas and apparently read the scowl on his face. "I don't know. It's up to your *grossdaddi*."

Thomas's gaze bounced about the too-comforting kitchen, skipping past the too-lovely woman to land on his granddaughter's hopeful face. "We'll see…"

Publishers Weekly bestselling author **Jocelyn McClay** grew up on an Iowa farm, ultimately pursuing a degree in agriculture. She met her husband while weight lifting in a small town—he "spotted" her. After thirty years in business management, they moved to an acreage in southeastern Missouri to be closer to family when their oldest of three daughters made them grandparents. When not writing, she keeps busy grandparenting, hiking, biking, gardening, quilting, knitting and substitute teaching.

Books by Jocelyn McClay

Love Inspired

Visit the Author Profile page at LoveInspired.com.

The Amish Spinster's Dilemma

Jocelyn McClay

LOVE INSPIRED
INSPIRATIONAL ROMANCE

LOVE INSPIRED®
INSPIRATIONAL ROMANCE

ISBN-13: 978-1-335-58651-3

The Amish Spinster's Dilemma

Copyright © 2023 by Jocelyn Ord

For questions and comments about the quality of this book, please contact us at CustomerService@Harlequin.com.

Love Inspired
22 Adelaide St. West, 41st Floor
Toronto, Ontario M5H 4E3, Canada
www.LoveInspired.com

Printed in U.S.A.

And the second is like unto it,
Thou shalt love thy neighbour as thyself.
—*Matthew* 22:39

First and always, I thank God
for this opportunity. This book is dedicated to
my mom and others who live with arthritis.

Chapter One

She was being watched.

The girl was back again. She peeked from behind one of the trees at the edge of the yard. Her pale face above an oversize dark coat was visible against the woods' hint of green, as the leaves debated whether or not to unfurl. Winter, as usual, was reluctant to release its grip on Wisconsin. But today, at least, held a promise of spring.

Emma Beiler kept her attention on the needle she was pushing through the woven golden straw. She mainly stitched hats with her treadle sewing machine, but the April day had lured her out on the porch to enjoy the sunshine after the long winter. Although sunny, it was still cool enough that Emma appreciated the sweater she wore. Cool enough that her fingers were complaining.

Securing the needle, she sighed and flexed her hands. Lately it seemed they were always complaining. Setting the unfinished hat on her lap, she stretched against the stiffness in her finger joints. Hopefully summer would be better, but there was no more denying it. The arthritis that she'd watched her *mamm* struggle with was taking hold of her. At least she was older than her mother was when it began its advance, although her mother might've silently borne the affliction for years before Emma had noticed. She stroked one particularly aching joint. How long before arthritis affected her livelihood as a hatmaker?

Her lips twitched in a rueful smile. Was forty-five young or old? Some days she felt young, some days old. Some days her mind felt one way while her body felt another. Or vice versa. Her smile faded. Regardless of how her mind or body felt, Emma knew old was in the title she and her twin sister, Elizabeth, shared. Followed by maids. Not a desirable description in an Amish community. "Single sister" wasn't much better. Another was "undiscovered treasures." Was undiscovered the same as overlooked? Emma pursed her lips. She'd been overlooked all her life. Overlooked by all but *Gott* it seemed. Surely it wasn't wishing for too much to want to be "discovered" by this stage?

But after a childhood of hand-me-downs and never having anything new, her least favorite term was "leftover blessings."

At least Elizabeth had a serious beau at one time so she'd known what it was like to feel wanted for herself. But not Emma.

Not a line of thought she wanted to venture down. Not again anyway. Besides, as was said in the *Biewel*, she was to be content whatever the circumstance. All the more reason to wonder about the furtive girl instead. Emma couldn't guess how old the child was from this distance. Nine? Ten? Eleven? Never having had children, she wasn't the best judge of their ages. Though the distance and the way the child darted behind trees and bushes made it difficult, Emma could tell the girl was already as tall as her own five foot nothing, or would be soon.

She'd shown up two days ago. Or at least that was the first time Emma had seen her. The deep blue of her attire against the still-naked winter woods had been as obvious to Emma as a blemish in the woven straw she constantly worked with. Another thing that was obvious was the girl's curiosity. That, along with the sun, had drawn Emma to work outside. To see how curious the girl would get. Because Emma was curious too. Curious why this girl, whatever her age, wasn't in school with other local Amish children.

At least—due to the girl's dress, black stockings and prayer *kapp* that dangled from the back of the girl's head—Emma thought she was Amish. Setting the unfinished hat on the arm of her chair, she rose, picked up her nearby cup of coffee and entered the house. After pouring herself a refill, she retrieved a plate from the cupboard and loaded it with the cookies Elizabeth had made yesterday, stacking the pile high enough that it would definitely be seen from a distance. It was more than she could eat, but they weren't for her. They were bait for the watcher.

Returning to the porch, she set her cup on the small table beside her chair and the loaded plate of cookies on the porch rail. After making much ado over selecting a cookie, she settled back into her chair. Facing the lane, she took an exaggerated bite of the snickerdoodle as she watched the dark-clad figure from the corner of her eye.

Emma hid her smile behind her cup as the girl left the cover of the woods to dash across the open yard and duck behind the laundry she'd hung out earlier that day. Humming a song remembered from when, as a hopeful young woman, she'd attended Sunday night singings decades ago, she chose another cookie, making a production of eating that one as well.

Dusting the crumbs from her fingers, Emma picked up the unfinished hat, automatically shifting it in her hands to retrieve the needle, and began to work again. *I won't be needing any supper if I eat another cookie, that's for sure and certain. But if it entices my shy friend closer, there are worse things to eat than Elizabeth's cookies.*

The girl darted from the clothesline to the edge of the house, out of Emma's sight. It was like trying to coax a bunny closer. Emma continued to hum as she worked. A short while later, she spied the girl peeking through the porch railings.

"Help yourself," she offered calmly without looking up from her work. "I think there're chocolate crinkles in the house if you'd rather have those. But I like these better." The girl didn't move from where she hovered at the edge of the porch. "My sister is *gut* at baking cookies. At least she always says so. Why don't you try them both and you can tell me what you think?"

The girl cocked her head as if she didn't understand Emma's words. With a raised eyebrow, Emma repeated them in English as opposed to the language the Amish used amongst themselves.

The girl looked like she could use a cookie or two, she was so thin. And a bath wouldn't go amiss either. If she'd come through the woods and across the creek beyond it, the streaks of mud on her face and stockings, visible as the girl inched her way closer, weren't surprising.

Staying on the other side of the porch, the girl snagged a cookie from the plate. Through the white railings, her cautious blue eyes watched Emma as she devoured the first cookie and reached for another.

Emma continued in English. "Well, do I have to tell my sister she's right about her baking skills, or do you want to try the chocolate crinkle cookies too, just to make sure?"

The blue eyes narrowed as the girl munched, before she spoke around a mouthful of cookie. "I better make sure."

Emma nodded as she set her work aside and rose from the chair. "That's wise. I'd do the same thing myself." Pausing at the door, she looked back to see the girl was now perched on the front steps. "Do you want something to drink as well? I can offer coffee or milk, but if you're not interested in either of those and you have a minute, I can make some hot chocolate."

The girl's eyes rounded with interest. Her slender throat bobbed as she hastily swallowed. "That'd be good."

With another nod, Emma entered the house, leaving the door open behind her. She raised her eyebrows as she lit the gas stove under the teakettle. The girl had responded in English. Unhesitating English. Amish children spoke the dialect of their parents at home and usually didn't learn English until they entered school. This girl hadn't responded to *Deitsch*, but was quite comfortable, it seemed, with English. Interesting.

Returning to the porch, Emma handed the girl a small plate of chocolate crinkle cookies. "Do you want to come in while the water is heating? Spring seems to be taking its time arriving at Miller's Creek. Even with the sunshine, it's still a bit nippy outside. At least, I think so."

Selecting one of the powdered sugarcoated cookies, the girl eyed her warily. "Then why were you working out here?"

Emma stifled a laugh. "Because I was wanting to get outside after the long winter." Deciding candor deserved candor, she continued. "And I wanted to see if you'd come any closer if I did."

The girl's lips twitched as if she too was suppressing a smile.

"So now that I've done both, are you interested in coming into the kitchen where it's a bit warmer?" Emma glanced down at the girl's mud-caked shoes. "If you take those off, that is."

The girl eyed the black stockings that were streaked up to her knees with mud. "Can I take off the socks as well?"

Emma smothered a sigh as she looked through the doorway to the gleaming linoleum floor of her kitchen. "Probably a good idea."

The girl needed no further encouragement. She dropped to the porch floor and tugged off her shoes and socks. To Emma's surprise, the youngster picked up the soiled articles and set them neatly along the railing. Wiggling her bare toes, she ambled through the door, carrying the plate of cookies. Setting it on the counter and shedding her oversize coat to hang it over the back of a chair, she glanced about the small but tidy house.

"I looked in the window." She nodded toward the attached two-car garage that held Emma's combination workshop and sales room. "Are you the Mad Hatter or something?"

Emma smiled as she shook her head. The girl was a character. Whoever she belonged to—Emma didn't recognize her as a child from the district—had their hands full. "Or something," she agreed, opening the connecting door to the shop and gesturing the girl inside. "I make and sell hats for our district, as well as a few other ones nearby." She raised an eyebrow. "I take it you didn't grow up as Amish?"

Strolling to a nearby shelf, the girl reached out to run a finger along a hat's brim. "No. I don't know if I'm Amish or not. But my grandpa wants me to be." She shrugged. "If I don't like it, I'll run away. 'Cause so far, it just seems like a bunch of rules."

From back in the kitchen, the sputter of the teakettle kept Emma from sputtering something herself. Returning to the stove, she turned off the burner. Retrieving two cups, she emptied a packet of hot chocolate mix into each. The girl stepped into the kitchen in time to see her tap the last bit from the packet into the crockery before adding water.

"You get hot chocolate from a box? I thought Amish made everything from scratch?"

The spoon scraped against the cup as Emma slowly stirred. "Did you see any cocoa beans out there while you were spying on me?"

The girl shook her head.

"Then I guess we don't make everything from scratch." She handed over one of the cups of steaming cocoa.

"Where are you from?"

The girl waved in the general direction of the small stand of woods and swampy creek beyond it. Emma furrowed her brows, trying to think of families in that area who might have children or grandchildren.

"What's your name?"

"I go by Cilla, but my real name," the girl sighed heavily, "is Priscilla Reihl."

Emma froze. Her heart clenched at the name. Priscilla had been the name of her best friend growing up. They'd been inseparable. Until one Sunday night when Priscilla had blushingly confessed that Thomas Reihl was giving her a ride home after the singing. The ride was the first of many, followed by a wedding as soon as Priscilla was old enough to marry. Still, as Thomas lived on the next farm over, she and Priscilla had stayed as close as a quilt top and backing with a thin batting; the beautiful Priscilla being the decorative top, Emma the serviceable and coordinating backing. It would've been easy to be jealous, but Priscilla had been as lovely inside as she'd been on the surface. Emma had cared for her through her illness four years ago and had been glad to help her lifelong friend. She still missed her daily.

"It's nice to meet you, Cilla." Emma haltingly probed, "You don't care for your name…?"

Cilla shrugged bony shoulders. "I was named for my grandma. I never met her."

Emma's eyes widened. It could be a coincidence. Having started centuries ago with a few families, the Amish had many surnames in common. Thomas Reihl had sons, though none now lived at home. All three had moved to the larger Amish settlement of Shipshewana, Indiana, to work in the RV factories. The two oldest were married. But neither of them was old enough to have a child Cilla's age. Unless…

"What was your *mamm*'s name?" Emma was speaking so slowly, the girl had cause to wonder at her intelligence. Because she could only think of one child of her good friend who might be old enough to parent the girl standing in her kitchen.

"Lena." The girl's expression clouded. For a moment, Emma wondered if she was going to cry, but her lips flattened into a firm line and her stick-thin arms stiffened as she fisted her hands. The slender shoulders again lifted, this time in a heavy sigh. "My mom had an aneursomething and died. They sent me to live with my grandpa. After they could find me, that is. I ran away… I didn't want to go live with somebody I'd never met and who couldn't have been bothered enough to see my mom." Her lower lip trembled for a moment before the movement was squelched. "Or me."

"I…see." And Emma did. Lena was Priscilla's eldest child. Her only daughter. The one who'd left Emma's friend heartbroken when the girl had departed Amish life for the *Englisch* as a teenager. *After* she'd been baptized into the church. Leaving before baptism was one thing. Part of *rumspringa* or the "run-around" years, as well as choosing a mate, was deciding whether the youth would be baptized into the church. If a *youngie* chose baptism, as most of the Amish youth did, it was understood there'd be no leaving the community after that decision. Leaving after baptism was like closing the door of no return, as she would've been shunned if she had. After Lena had taken off, Priscilla had spent many hours at Emma's home crying before she'd dried her tears and collected herself enough to return home and care for her husband and younger boys.

Her thoughts whirling, Emma startled at the clatter of hooves coming up her lane. Schooling herself to enter the hat shop and greet a customer, she jolted at rapid knocking on the kitchen door. Jumping up, she opened it to find her neighbor Thomas, his normally reserved face taut with worry, his hands clasped tightly enough the weathered knuckles showed in sharp relief.

"*Guder Daag.* I'm sorry to bother you but have you seen…" His voice trailed away when he spied the young girl seated at the table. "Priscilla." The name was spoken in a relieved sigh.

"Cilla," the girl corrected with a mutinous expression, before shifting in her chair to stare at Emma's kitchen wall in an obvious attempt to block the man out.

Emma's brows rose at the girl's action. Her gaze swiveled back to Thomas. His jaw tightened. Above the brown beard that indicated he'd been married, his face was flushed. Blue eyes, ones Emma had always admired for the way they'd looked with adoration upon her friend, were glazed with a desperation that Emma had never seen before.

An awkward silence filled the room. Under the weight of it, Emma hustled to the stove to reheat the water. "Come in, Thomas. We were just having some cocoa. Why don't you join us for a cup."

Frowning, he blinked at her. Emma dumped cocoa mix into a cup. Thomas had probably never sat down during a work day unless it was to grab a bite for lunch, or for some other dire necessity. Glancing at Cilla, who was staring pointedly at the unadorned wall, Emma figured the current situation qualified.

"Sit," she mouthed to him, tipping her head toward the table, then toward the silent girl.

Thomas opened his mouth before apparently determining silence might be a better course of action. Dipping his chin in acknowledgment, he warily approached the table, much as he might an unpredictable animal. "*Ja.* Some hot cocoa sounds *gut.*"

The clanking of the spoon against the cup was the only sound as Emma stirred the cocoa on her way to setting it down in front of Thomas. "I'm surprised you made it across the creek, Cilla. There's usually a good bit of water in it during the spring." Easing into her chair, Emma lifted her own cup.

To her relief, the girl responded. "I found some rocks and stayed on them." Cilla glanced down at her bare legs. She wiggled her toes. "For the most part."

"You shouldn't be trying to cross—"

Seeing the girl's shoulders stiffen, Emma kicked Thomas's boot under the table. He halted the admonition. What Cilla needed right now was a connection, not a scolding.

"I played in that creek a lot with your grandmother when we were young. But it's much better in summer when you can go barefoot and don't have to worry about your shoes or stockings."

Cilla swiveled enough to look at Emma with

raised eyebrows. "My grandma played in that creek?"

"Oh, *ja*. We were like little beavers, building temporary dams when we weren't having stick races."

The girl twisted completely in her chair to face Emma. And, by default, her grandfather. "Stick races?"

"*Ja*. To see whose stick could float down the creek the fastest." Emma shook her head with a mock woebegone expression. "She always won."

Emma couldn't curb a quick glance toward Thomas. Priscilla had won him as well. Without even trying. Emma had loved her neighbor ever since she'd first seen him across the creek, helping with bales of hay that were almost as big as he was. But from the first day she and her best friend had entered school, he never had eyes for anyone but Priscilla.

So Emma had built walls to contain her love for her best friend's beau. She'd had years to do so. She'd braced the walls up after every Sunday night singing, when Priscilla would wave as she went out the door with Thomas and Emma would be left to go home alone. She'd fortified them when she'd seen Thomas on his wedding day, beholding Priscilla in her new blue dress with all the love in his eyes that Emma had secretly dreamed would be directed toward her. She'd bolstered them further when Lena was born, and Thomas had looked upon his wife and *dochter* with wonder, as if he couldn't believe they were his. As Emma had longed to be. But to feel that way was a betrayal to her friend. So the walls were built, and after forty years of construction and patching, they were insurmountable.

She'd made a promise to Priscilla before her friend had passed. But she'd made a promise to herself as well. The walls would stay in place. Thomas was not really free. To Emma, he would always be Priscilla's husband. As he'd closed himself off since she'd died, it was evident Thomas felt the same way. Although she'd attempted to help her widowed neighbor, he'd held her at arm's length.

"I think she found sticks as slender and quick as she was."

She had Cilla's full attention. The girl was smiling, which contrasted with Thomas's frown. Emma could feel the table vibrate as his leg bounced underneath it. He wouldn't stay much longer. "There's an empty container on the counter. Why don't you take home some of whichever cookies you liked best." Emma winked at the girl. "Then maybe I can get my sister to make more."

Cilla rose to do as requested. But as she passed, Emma heard her mutter, "It's not my home."

Thomas heard the girl's mutter as well. His hand tightened around the cup of cocoa he hadn't really tasted. Hot chocolate wasn't going to fix the situation he'd found himself in when an unknown girl had been dropped on his doorstep. He pushed to his feet when Cilla returned to the table, the expression that faced him much less sweet than the cookies she carried. Emma shook her head as she eyed them both, but her gaze remained on him when she spoke.

"*Ach*, I forgot the hat outside. Cilla, I don't suppose you'd get it from the porch?" When the girl nodded and turned toward the door, Emma continued, "Be careful. There's a needle in it."

Cilla was barely through the door when Emma murmured, "It's all right to ask for help, Thomas. But whether you ask or not, I'm going to give it to you. Because you truly need it."

He had no time to respond before the girl came bounding in again. "This is cool." Cilla handed the unfinished hat to Emma. "Would you teach me how to do it?"

"*Ja*. But not today. I think your grandfather wants to get back to work."

Scowling, Cilla retrieved her coat from the back of the chair and went out the door. Slinging the coat over her shoulder, she snagged her shoes and stockings from the porch. Emma and Thomas watched as she hopped in bare feet through the yard to Thomas's rig, pausing only to give the horse a quick pat before she scrambled up into the buggy.

"Well, she won't have any problem going barefoot as the weather warms up," Emma observed with a smile.

Thomas only grunted as he picked up the container of cookies. After a nod to Emma, he left the house to trudge to his buggy and climb in. He felt the girl's—Cilla, he needed to think of her as Cilla—intense attention on his actions as he gathered up the lines and headed the horse back down the lane. Once they were on the way, Cilla curled her bare feet up under her and stared out the side window so she wouldn't have to glimpse her unwanted *grossdaddi*. Thomas sighed quietly.

Silence could be deafening. He was used to silence after his wife had died and, one by one, his sons had left to find work elsewhere. But silence when someone was right beside you, intentionally ignoring you, had a way of roaring. Unlike the quiet when you were alone.

Even with two people living in it again, the silence in his home had been roaring lately.

He directed the gelding across the low water bridge. The horse bobbed its head uneasily at the sound of the water rushing through the culverts under his feet. Thomas looked from the water level in the creek to the girl beside him and raised his eyebrows. It was surprising she'd made it across the creek with only her shoes and socks to suffer for it, but he remembered the passage with the rocks as well.

When she'd been alive, Priscilla had used it numerous times to visit her friend when she chose not to drive the pony cart Thomas had built her for the trip. The farms were right across the twenty-foot-wide creek from each other. But to get there by buggy, one had to take a longer route by road before eventually crossing the creek at the low water bridge. On foot, it was much quicker to cross the creek if it was passable. But sometimes it wasn't and trying to do so could be dangerous. He glanced again at the girl and her folded muddy legs just visible under one of his sons' old jackets. He needed to warn her, but perhaps Emma was right. He should find something to say other than reprimands. Thomas rubbed the back of his neck with one hand as he urged the gelding to a faster speed to reach the solace of his shop.

He might be unwanted by Cilla, but she wasn't unwanted by him. Thomas ran his gaze over the strawberry-hinted blond hair that drooped from its pins, threatening to tumble all the way down over her shoulders. With her blue eyes and delicate features, Cilla looked like her *mamm*, his *dochter*, Lena. Who in turn, had looked very much like her *mamm,* Priscilla. Thomas squeezed his eyes shut against a welling of grief. *Ja*, he wanted Cilla. He just didn't know what to do with her. Which was why he'd sent a letter to his married sons in Shipshewana to see if they could take her in. They would know what to do with a child more so than he. His daughters-in-law could teach her to cook and run a household and all the things an Amish woman needed to know. There would eventually be other children in their families for the girl to interact with. It would be a *gut* life for her. *Ja*, it was best for all if she joined them in Shipshe. And when she left, it would take this roaring silence back to a quiet silence. He grimaced. A much too quiet silence.

Thomas's shoulders lifted in a heavy sigh. But in the meantime, Emma was right. He needed her help. Something he definitely didn't want. He had nothing against Emma. She'd always been there across the creek as long as he could remember. With her brown hair and eyes—Emma had fine brown eyes—she was a pleasant-looking woman. He was surprised someone hadn't married her years ago. But every time he saw her, he thought of his wife. They'd been inseparable. Like the two pieces of twine that, in parallel, held a bale of hay together. When one strand was missing, the bale came apart completely. Like he had when his *fraa* had died. He couldn't see Emma without holding his breath for a moment, hoping Priscilla would walk in as well.

The girl was still determinedly turned away from him. *Nee*, he didn't want Emma's help, but until his granddaughter went to live with one of his married sons, he needed it.

Chapter Two

The girl was back the next day.

Cilla, Emma reminded herself. Her name was Cilla. It was easier to think of her as that instead of her full name, Priscilla. Every time she thought of that name, a ripple of grief swept through her. The Amish way was not to mourn overmuch, for to do so could be questioning God's plan. Emma didn't question His plan, even in her loneliness at being single, but she did miss her friend.

She smiled as she watched the girl dart from the woods. Cilla might have her *mamm*'s looks and her *grossmammi*'s name, but her personality was all her own. Priscilla had been everything that was sweet and feminine; dainty, demure and accommodating. Cilla looked to be inheriting her *grossdaddi*'s tall, lean frame. Along with *Deitsch*, demure didn't seem to be in her vocabulary. And, observing the *kapp* that once again bounced at the side of her head and the mud that smeared her stockings all the way up to her knees, she didn't appear to have too many feminine bones in her body. Emma's smile turned rueful. She was afraid she was already well on her way to loving the girl.

Just as she had been from the moment she'd first seen Cilla's grandfather. Of course, she'd only been five at the time. But she'd never been able to shake the longing. Although watching him fall in love with her best friend and watching Priscilla grow to reciprocate his feelings had taught her to stifle, corral and bury her love over the years. Bury it so deep that even thinking of him that way was like wanting a food that she knew she was highly allergic to. To deny was to protect.

Besides, she had a different role now. Priscilla had secured a pledge from Emma that she would take care of Thomas when she was gone. Emma had tried. Only to be rebuffed. How did you take care of someone who didn't want to be taken care of? If he noticed, he never commented on the fact that his house was cleaned on a regular basis.

She supposed he ate the meals she dropped by. The empty dishes made their way back to her porch a few days after she'd left them in his kitchen. Initially when making a delivery, she'd stick her head into his blacksmith shop before she departed. Deciding after a while that, for all the attention he paid her, she might as well have been talking to his anvil, she now just left the food on the kitchen counter. The few times she'd caught him retreating from the porch after returning a clean dish, he'd looked embarrassed, but hale and hearty, so she figured whenever he'd found the food, it hadn't been so late that he'd contracted food poisoning.

Emma's lips twitched as she opened the outside door of the shop to greet the girl. This time though, Thomas might be a little more receptive to her assistance.

"Did you leave any dirt in the creek?"

Cilla looked up from where she was shucking off her shoes and stockings. "Yeah. Mostly. Someday, I'll make it all the way over on the rocks."

"There's still a good bit of mud around there even if you stay on the rocks. Sometimes the creek can be more swamp than running water. Sometimes it moves so fast and high it flows right over the bridge on the road."

Cilla paused in wiping her bare feet on the mat by the door. "Really?"

"*Ja.* Really. So your grandfather was right. You need to be careful around the creek."

Cilla scowled as she entered the shop.

"I don't suppose he knows you're here?" Emma had her answer when the girl's scowl deepened. "If you tell him that you're leaving and where you're going, it might not be considered running away. To my mind, that would be a good habit to break."

Cilla hunched a shoulder. "He doesn't care. He didn't want me anyway." The words were offhand but her expression wasn't.

Emma's lips tipped into a compassionate smile. "Did he tell you that?"

"No. But he didn't have to. He never acts like he cares. I thought he'd fall down from shock when the lady brought me to his door."

"Hmm. I'm sure it was a surprise. And I'm sure he cares more than you think. He loved your *grossmammi* very much. Your mother as well."

Cilla shrugged again. It seemed to be the language the girl was most comfortable with. She wandered over to pick up an unfinished hat from where it sat with others on the bench near the treadle sewing machine. "Can you show me how to make one of these?"

Accepting the change of subject, Emma followed her over. "For sure and certain I can, but I think maybe your first lesson should be your own *kapp*." She gestured toward the girl's dangling prayer covering. "Would you mind?"

When Cilla shook her head, causing the *kapp* to flop further, Emma freed it from the girl's drooping hair. "It helps to get your hair secured first. Always *gut* to have a firm foundation to build on. I have a brush in the house, as well as a few more pins. I'll show you how I do it. Sound *gut*?"

Cilla shrugged. But Emma saw an emphatic yes. She led the way from the shop, through the house and into her bedroom. Her cat, mostly black with a white nose, chest and four feet, stretched from where she'd been reclining on the quilt-covered bed.

"You have a cat?"

"Is that what she is? I thought for a while she was a squirrel." Emma left Cilla eyeing the resettling cat as she retrieved a brush from the top of her dresser.

Cilla giggled. "What's her name?"

Emma freed the girl's hair from the remainder of the pins and started to brush the upper-back-length tresses. "Willow."

"That's a weird name."

"I found her under a willow tree by the creek when she was a kitten." Emma searched the dresser until she found what she was looking for, two large barrettes, last used many years back. Securing them in the cuff of her sleeve and the ponytail holder on her wrist, she returned to brushing Cilla's hair. She had to clear the emotion from her throat as she ran the brush a final time through the blond strands with their hints of strawberry.

"Your *grossmammi* and I used to put up each other's hair when we were younger. You have the same color as she did."

"Really?" The girl straightened her shoulders. "My mom had this color too."

"I know."

"You knew my mom?"

"When she was younger like you. Until her teenage years. She was tall like your *grossdaddi*. Like it appears you're going to be."

The hair in Emma's hand shifted slightly as Cilla apparently made a face.

"I don't know that I want to be like my gross…gross dad."

Perusing the part running down the center of the girl's hair, Emma winced at the comment. "I think, if you let yourself, you'll discover he has some very *gut* qualities. At least your *grossmammi* thought so, and she was a very special woman." Emma worried her bottom lip briefly before shifting from empathetic to a businesslike tone.

"You need to pull your hair back from your face and behind your ears, where you secure it on both sides with barrettes." She did so as she spoke. "Then you secure it tightly in a ponytail close to the head. You have enough hair that you'll want to double it over so you can roll it up into a nice, tight bun. You stabilize it with some hair pins." Emma continued working as she spoke. Cilla's attention was still fastened on Willow, who watched them lazily from the bed.

Retrieving a hairnet from the top of the dresser, Emma tucked one end under the bun. "You can keep this net. It helps secure your hair when you're active. And you, my new friend, seem like a very active girl. I put mine on back-to-front, twist it, then return it front-to-back. Secure the bun in the net and the bun and net to the head. And now you're all ready for your…" Emma glanced at the grimy *kapp* she'd set on the dresser. "For one of my *kapps* for the time being. We'll get you a few new ones from the store later."

Placing one of her extra *kapps* over Cilla's secured bun, she attached it with a couple of pins. Cilla reached up to touch the arrangement with tentative fingers.

"There's a mirror in the bathroom. Why

don't you go in and see what it looks like so you know what you're aiming for."

The girl hastened to do so. Emma trailed after her to the small room, smiling as the girl craned her head one way and another as she studied herself in the tiny mirror.

"Wow. I look different." Cilla touched her hands to the *kapp* again.

Emma smiled. "Probably best to touch your *kapp* as seldom as possible. White picks up dirt, so they aren't the easiest thing to keep clean or to iron either with all the pleats. Although our *kapps* don't have as many pleats as some."

"Aren't they all the same?"

"No. Different communities have different *kapps*. Even the men's hats can be different. The brims of the men's hats in our district are wider than some of the neighboring ones."

Cilla furrowed her brow. "That's kind of weird."

Emma's smile widened. "It depends on what the district's *Ordnung* states. The *Ordnung* is the set of rules that the local church lives by."

"Is that where it says you have to wear this kind of thing?"

"No. That's from the *Biewel*. The Bible says women are to cover their heads when praying, and as we are to pray without ceasing, we always keep our heads covered." She winked at Cilla. "But sometimes in the summer when I'm working in the garden, I wear a scarf or handkerchief. Come on, we'll give you a chance to practice getting it up this way."

They returned to the bedroom. Carefully this time, Cilla unpinned her *kapp* and set it on the dresser. "What's different, besides the pleats?"

"Hmm." Emma pursed her lips as she recalled *kapps* from other districts. "Some have more starch, some less. Some tie their ribbons, some do not. As teenage girls, we kept our ribbons untied and used them to flirt with the teenage boys." Wearing a one-sided grin, she demonstrated by twirling the end of one of her ribbons. "Although properly demure, your *grossmammi* was very good at it. Not that she had to be, as the boys flocked to her anyway. But she only had eyes for your *grossdaddi*, and he only had eyes for her."

Cilla scowled. "He must've been a lot less grouchy then."

"Your *grossdaddi* was quite fun. Once."

"Really?" Cilla furrowed her brow, as if she'd have to see the phenomenon to believe it. And even then it might be doubtful.

"Really. He just misses your *grossmammi*,

and he takes a while to warm up to change. And you're definitely a big change."

The girl's lips trembled briefly before her nostrils flared and her jaw firmed. "I've had a big change too."

"*Ja*. For sure and certain, you have." Her heart aching, Emma refrained from pulling the girl into her arms as she longed to. It was too soon, and Cilla was obviously too determined to handle things on her own. "What do you think might be a *gut* thing about being here?"

Cilla wrinkled her nose. Her gaze shot to where Willow was curled on the bed, watching them through amber eyes. "The animals?"

Emma leaned over the bed to gather her unresisting cat into her arms. "You say it like it's a question. Do you or don't you like the animals?" She held Willow so Cilla could pet the purring feline.

"I do." As she stroked a hand down the cat's sleek black back, the girl's response was emphatic.

"Well, then, why aren't you working with them?"

"My granddad won't let me."

"Won't let you? Or doesn't know you want to?" The way Cilla's eyes slid away told Emma it was the latter. "Well, that's something we'll have to work on then." When Willow signaled she was ready to get down, Emma bent and turned her loose on the floor. Her cat wanted to be petted, purred like a diesel generator running an Amish furniture shop, but only tolerated being held on her terms.

"In the meantime, let's have you put up your own hair."

Cilla tried, for a short frustrating time. Watching the girl's face grow more and more dismayed, Emma gently took the brush and pins from her hands and redid Cilla's bun and *kapp* herself. "It can be hard to learn on your own hair, but you'll get the hang of it soon. How about you practice once on mine so you can see what you're doing."

Emma glanced out the window to ensure no customers had arrived while she'd been distracted. Seeing no buggies in the yard, she began to undo her hair. When she unwound the net and pulled out the pins and ponytail holder, the dark brown strands tumbled down to dangle against her dress well below her hips.

"Wow." Cilla exclamation was extended with awe. "That's long."

Stifling a moment of pride, for being *hochmut* was counter to their culture, Emma ran the brush through her hair a few times. For a reason she couldn't define, she wasn't ready for someone else to brush it. Beyond herself, her *mamm* and her sister, it was something only Priscilla had ever done. "It's never been cut."

"Never?"

"Never."

"Another Be Well thing?"

Emma's lips twitched. "*Ja*. The *Biewel* encourages us to not cut our hair."

Cilla's face clouded. "My mom cut hers."

Emma handed the girl the ponytail holder and brush. "I imagine she had her reasons while living with the *Englisch*. Now, let's see how it goes getting mine back up. Since it's longer, where we doubled yours once, I usually double mine four times."

"Wow," Cilla repeated reverently.

Thomas cleared the edge of the woods and started across the yard. It was quicker to cross the creek by foot instead of harnessing his horse and driving along the road. He figured the girl had traveled the same way. *If* she'd traveled this way. His stride hitched momentarily at the thought that she might not have. If not, then where would she be? Would he be able to find her? *Nee*, she'd seemed to like Emma yesterday. She had to be here. If only she'd quit disappearing.

It would be easier if she was busy in school. But Bishop Weaver and he had agreed, as school would be out in a month and the girl didn't seem to understand *Deitsch*, it might be better for her to wait until the fall to start. But what if they were wrong? He was obviously a master at making poor choices regarding his *kin*. None of them had stayed around. He sighed. This was for the best. Probably. Hopefully. By fall, the girl would be starting school in Shipshe anyway.

Striding past the house, he glanced in the window. And froze in his tracks. Standing in profile to him was Emma, with her hair streaming down her back. Thomas realized his mouth was hanging open when he found himself needing to swallow. He'd never seen a woman other than his wife with her hair down. Emma looked...different than she normally did. Normally, Emma Beiler sometimes reminded him of a little brown wren. But there was nothing wren-like about this Emma. Swallowing again, he forced his feet into motion. At least his glance in the window had answered one question. Priscilla was here. *Nee*, not Priscilla. He was too used to associating Emma with Priscilla. Cilla. Cilla was here. Rounding the corner of the porch, Thomas frowned. He'd come for the one question. Now that he was here, a few more were troubling him.

On the porch, Thomas gave the door two

slow raps. Normally, that would've been followed by opening it and walking in. Before and particularly during his marriage to Priscilla, they'd been those kinds of neighbors. It'd been as if the Beiler residence was her residence as well. Since she was gone, he'd made efforts not to go inside the house. Today, envisioning that long, dark flow of hair, he stayed firmly rooted on the porch.

"Just a moment!" Emma's distant voice sounded flustered. A short bit later, it was Cilla who opened the door to him.

Thomas stared for a moment at her with her hair and *kapp* neatly fixed. At the sight of Emma's unbound glory, although he'd noted his granddaughter was in the room, he hadn't really looked at her. Now he did. His lips framed her mother's name, Lena, before he caught himself.

"You look…" He cleared his throat and nodded at her. Although it felt like trying to crack the ice in the creek before the frozen water was ready to yield, he forced the corners of his mouth up. He must've succeeded somewhat, as her fierce frown upon seeing him softened slightly as she reached up to touch her head.

Emma hustled into the room, her hands pinning her *kapp* to her hair as she walked. Thomas had never noticed before how, although quick and efficient, Emma always moved with grace. Flushing slightly, he suddenly found the cat ambling along behind her much more interesting than he'd ever considered a feline. Particularly one in the house.

Cilla retreated from the doorway to allow Emma to step into it.

"Thomas. I'm glad you're here."

Well, that made one of them.

Emma clasped her hands together with a pop that almost made Thomas jump. "Didn't you mention you were needing a new hat this spring?"

He furrowed his eyebrows. *"Nee."*

Emma glanced significantly at where Cilla was kneeling on the linoleum, currently absorbed with petting the cat. "That's what I thought I'd understood."

He followed her gaze. "Oh. *Ja.*"

"While Cilla and Willow entertain each other, why don't you see if there's something here that might suit you?" She strode briskly to the shop door. Hesitantly, he followed her through it.

When she closed the door firmly behind him, he frowned. "Why don't we just not speak in English? She doesn't seem to understand our dialect."

Emma pursed her lips as she automatically

went to straighten a stack of hats. "Sometimes I wonder. Is that why she's not in school?"

Thomas took off his hat to examine it. He fingered a spot that threatened to wear through. Maybe he did need a new one, but not today. He was just fine as he was. He twisted the hat in his hands by its brim. "Partly. It would certainly be easier for me. But for her, it seemed almost too big of a change. She certainly doesn't need it to learn English, as many of our Amish youth do. The bishop said it was all right to wait until fall to start. When everything's not so…much." He twisted the hat faster. "If she's still here."

"What do you mean?" Emma spun to face him.

"I reached out to my married sons in Shipshewana to see if they'll take her in. They and their wives would have a much better chance of making a home for her than I would."

"Oh, Thomas." She shook her head at him.

He scowled. "What do you mean, 'oh, Thomas'?" he mimicked her tone.

"*You* need to make an effort to make a home for her."

"I don't have time to." *I don't know how to.*

"You don't have time not to. She's always welcome here. But do you like interrupting your day to keep coming over to find her?"

She flinched fractionally at his deepened scowl, which tacitly stated the obvious. "Then you need to find some way to connect. Make it feel like home and she won't unexpectedly take off so much."

"Doing what?"

Emma shrugged. "She likes animals. Let her help with the livestock chores."

Crossing his arms over his chest, his face creased into the comfortable lines of another scowl. No wonder it'd felt like it would crack when he'd tried a smile.

"Try it. Could it make the situation any worse?"

Thomas wanted to tell her yes. What if he was the reason Lena had left all those years ago? He ran his fingers through his beard, wishing for the millionth time that Priscilla was here. Would letting Cilla help him with the livestock make the situation worse? He supposed not. It would only have the roaring silence follow them out to the barn. It and his shop were now his sanctuaries, where silence, other than the expected, comforting sounds found there, was just silence.

"Are you going to try?"

Why did he ever think of Emma as a wren? Although not of the flashy coloring, she was more of a woodpecker. Peck, peck, peck. She probably wouldn't leave him alone until he was a pile of sawdust.

"Do I have to report back?" His voice dripped with irony, much like the maple trees did when the sap started running in the spring.

Folding her arms over her chest, Emma smiled. "*Ja.* I think you do."

Chapter Three

Thomas flicked a glance to where Cilla was setting the table as he chiseled scorched potatoes from the bottom of the skillet, having just barely saved scrambled eggs from the same fate. At least the girl wasn't frowning. The silence between them wasn't deafening. It was more...mumbling. It was a relief. Her afternoon at Emma's was probably...*nee*, he admitted with a sigh, definitely the reason.

He'd left shortly after Emma had dragged him into the hat shop. Only staying long enough to step back into the house and admonish Cilla to not venture from the rocks when she forded the creek. Now that her hair wasn't covering her face, it'd been easy to see her roll her eyes at the unsolicited advice. Thomas tried not to let it bother him. Much. Lena hadn't rolled her eyes at him when she was a girl, but she'd left anyway. Maybe this was better. At least he knew where he stood.

Crossing the creek on the way home, he'd glanced toward where the water flattened out, upstream from the rocks, becoming more swamp-like among sporadic higher tufts of grass. Thomas frowned at a childhood memory of a cow that'd been lost in quicksand not a hundred yards beyond where he was traversing on the rocks. When they'd finally been able to pull the carcass from the sucking mud, they'd found part of a skeleton from a bovine lost, presumably to the same situation, years earlier. He'd fenced off that part of the pasture to keep his cows safe. In some moods, the creek could be fun. In others, it could be quite dangerous.

Grimacing, he shoveled blackened potatoes onto two plates alongside tired eggs. Emma Beiler could probably be the same. Not dangerous. But unsettling. He might as well try what she'd suggested. Try to find some way to connect with the girl. Besides, Emma would probably peck, peck, peck at him until he reported back that he had anyway.

Taking his seat, he offered a silent prayer of thanks, adding into it a request for wisdom with those who shared his table. When he said "amen" and opened his eyes, he was astonished to see Cilla had closed hers during the prayer as well, an unusual occurrence. The observation warmed him more than the over-heated stove he'd just left. With a choke hold on his utensils, he cleared his throat.

"I'm going back out to the barn tonight, after dinner." In his peripheral vision, he saw Cilla look up in surprise at his abrupt comment. Thomas took a deep breath. "From the way she's acting, I think the Jersey cow is going to have her calf. I usually stay out there with her to make sure she doesn't have issues." His attention on his plate, Thomas poked his fork through some burned slices of potato.

"If you want to come out with me, that's… fine." It wasn't fine, but Emma was right. It was probably…helpful. Not for him, but for them. Although the girl would probably refuse.

When he looked up with mock casualness, Thomas saw he had Cilla's full attention. He blinked at the way her face lit up like the morning sun peeking over the horizon in July.

"Really?"

"Ja." Even for him, the answer was slow. "That is, if you want to."

"I do. I want to. Can we go now?"

"Uh… Eat your supper first."

Cilla looked down at her plate and gri-maced. Thomas hid his own scowl when the girl stabbed at a potato and it shot off her plate.

She maneuvered a mouthful onto her fork and considered it a moment before sticking it into her mouth. Closing her eyes and scrunching up her nose, she gamely chewed.

Thomas stared at the wall as he crunched down on his own bite of burned potatoes. With a sigh, he stood and carried his plate to the sink. He turned back to the table in time to see Cilla frown as she stared at another bite she'd loaded onto her fork. He felt the closest kinship he'd had to her thus far. "How about a sandwich before we go?"

"It smells in here."

Thomas supposed it did. To him, they were *gut* smells. Fresh hay. Clean straw. Contented livestock. His shoulders tightened as he waited for the girl to turn around and go back to the house.

"I like it."

He pivoted to watch her as she paused in the barn doorway. Her eyes were bright. Her head swiveled from one direction to another as she took in the barn's interior. Surprisingly, her hair was still neat from when it'd been put up earlier. With only the briefest hesitation, Cilla headed for the line of horse stalls. The Belgians, their big heads almost half her size, eyed her curiously. The Standardbred retreated to the back of the stall, probably figuring anything with this much activity meant he'd soon have to go to work.

Thomas's lips twitched as he turned toward the cow's stall, approaching quietly to avoid stressing her if she was already restless with impending labor. She'd had calves before, and Thomas didn't expect any problems. Still, she was a good little cow, and it was better to be on hand just in case. She was lying with her feet tucked under her when he came to the wooden half wall of the stall. By the disturbances in the straw, he could tell she'd been up and down several times already. The calf should arrive soon.

He was prepared to advise Cilla to approach quietly as well. To his surprise, the girl silently appeared a few minutes later to lean her elbows on the half wall a few feet from him. The Jersey regarded them with her big brown eyes.

"She looks like a deer," Cilla observed in an awed whisper.

Thomas tilted his head. He supposed she did. Brown in color, Jerseys were a small dairy breed, known for high butterfat content in their milk.

"Does she have a name?"

Having obtained her as a calf, Thomas had never called her anything more than "the Jersey," "girl" or "cow." He shook his head. That seemed to be a satisfactory response for his companion as a smile lit up her face.

A while later, Cilla watched in amazement as the cow licked her newborn son. "He's beautiful! Can I name him?"

Thomas rubbed the back of his neck. He wasn't in the habit of naming anything except the horses so, while driving them, he could call out their name when needed, but he didn't see any reason not to name the new arrival. The girl had been amazingly quiet during the whole process, when he'd expected a barrage of distracting questions and chatter. He glanced at her profile. What would it hurt? Especially if it seemed to mean so much to her. His lips quirked. Connect, Emma had said. Who'd have thought it would've been over a calf?

"*Ja*. That'd be fine, I guess. Might as well name the cow too."

Cilla beamed like he'd given her the deed to the farm. Fisting her hand, she placed it on top of the stall's weathered board and rested her chin on it. "I'm going to call the new baby Bambi, and his mother is now Faline."

Thomas hiked his eyebrows. "Bambi?" he echoed. He'd been expecting something like Brownie or Bitsy. What kind of a name was Bambi?

"It's the name of a baby deer in a movie. And he looks like a baby deer."

He studied the newborn. The cream-colored calf did look like a fawn, only without the spots. Thomas ran his hand over his mouth, hiding a smile. If the new one remained a bull, he hoped the animal later forgave him for his name. "Bambi it is then."

He jerked when Cilla threw her arms around him in an exuberant hug. "Thanks!"

Thomas held very still, preternaturally aware of the thin arms about his waist as they watched the calf struggle to his feet. He was afraid to breathe. Afraid any movement would dislodge the slender arms from their position, removing them and the unexpected joy that their presence brought.

When Cilla dropped her arms and moved farther down the half wall to get a better view of the calf taking his first meal, Thomas drew a shaky inhale. Had he ever brought Lena out to see a new calf or foal? Or had he just assumed she wouldn't be interested and never asked, figuring she'd rather stay in the house with Priscilla? He'd brought the boys out to the barn from the moment they could walk. Would it have made a difference?

"Doesn't a barn need a cat? If Emma has a cat in the house, why don't you have a cat in the barn?" Cilla turned to him, her eyes round with excitement. "Or maybe get a cat for the house here."

"No cat in the house." He could barely keep it up as it was. And wouldn't have been able to if Emma didn't come over occasionally and clean. Something else he owed her for. Which he wished he didn't. But he'd never told her not to come. He frowned. And he'd never thanked her.

"Oh." Cilla's face fell.

Thomas still felt the ripples of joy that'd flooded through him at the spontaneous embrace of those slender arms. He scratched his chin. He supposed a cat in the barn made sense. It would help keep the mice population in check.

"The Zooks had some kittens a while back. Maybe they still have one they might be willing to part with."

When the words cut through the silence, Thomas looked around at the newly-dubbed Faline, the huge heads of his draft horses and Banner, his Standardbred, as if one of them had spoken. "Kittens" wasn't a word that was normally in his vocabulary. Neither was the thought of visiting a neighbor to see if he could get one.

"Really!" Eyes rounded, Cilla whirled toward him abruptly, drawing the attention of the new mother and calf in the stall.

He sighed. "*Ja.* We'll go tomorrow morning after chores."

Just as abruptly, the slender arms once again encircled his waist. Again, Thomas hesitated to breathe. Afraid to make a movement that would end this precious gift. A gift he hadn't realized he'd been so desperately needing. *Oh, Priscilla. I miss you. You could make her a home. You would know what to do with her.* He looked down at the strawberry blond hair, so like his wife's, that was pulled back under the smudged *kapp. And Priscilla, you would've so enjoyed having her here. I wish you were here now.*

Releasing her hug, Cilla returned to watching the youngster who was now exploring his new world. A smile split her narrow face. "I can't wait to tell Emma."

Thomas swallowed. That wasn't who he wished could be told. But he supposed he had her to thank for this moment. Maybe if Cilla had a cat to spend time with here, she'd spend less time across the creek with Emma. That'd be less time he'd have to spend there as well to fetch her. Although he was staring at the fawn-colored calf, Thomas was seeing an un-encumbered flow of long dark hair. A flush of guilt swept through him at thinking of any woman other than his wife. Less time with Emma Beiler would definitely be a *gut* thing.

Cilla was up almost as early as he was the next morning. Her hair didn't look as neat as it had the day before, but it was definitely an improvement from her earlier efforts. Following Thomas to the barn, she watched the calf while he did chores. Occasionally she'd prompt him to hurry just a little bit faster. Much too soon for Thomas's comfort, they pulled up to the Zooks' barn. Knowing where he'd find the dairy farmer this time of day, Thomas headed for the milking parlor with Cilla at his heels.

"Morning, Thomas!" Isaiah Zook rose from where he'd been milking a Holstein cow. "What brings you over? I haven't left anything at your blacksmith shop, have I?"

"Nee." Thomas rubbed his hand across his face, glad a portion of it was covered by a beard to conceal his blush. "I…uh…understand you might have some kittens."

Isaiah's gaze traveled from Thomas to the girl beside him. Cilla had her hands clasped before her mouth and was shifting weight from one foot to the other. The dairyman grinned. "I never figured you for a cat person, Thomas."

Thomas's face flamed further. "I never figured me for one either. But things have a way of changing when someone unexpectedly comes into your life."

"I'm sure Aaron here would agree with you." Isaiah nodded to the dark-haired man watching with interest as he released a cow from the stanchion on the other side of the parlor. "A few months back he came to the farm an unattached bachelor, and now in a few months he'll be a married man." The farmer turned his attention to Cilla. "Let's see if we can find a suitable match for you as well. The older *kin* have already left for school. The best one here to help you would be Joanne. She's usually playing with the kittens as we milk anyway. The litter was born in the hayloft, but when they got old enough, and with mama cat's permission, we moved them down to an empty oat bin. More accessible for the younger *kin*."

He nodded toward a wooden door down an alley that hung open. Wood slats filled the doorway about a third of the way up. Longing to stay with the men, Thomas nonetheless led Cilla over. Peering over the slats, he saw a little girl playing with several black-and-white kittens. She looked up at their arrival.

Thomas nodded toward Cilla. "My *kinskind*," he paused at the jolt that ran through him. Was that the first time he'd called her that? "She would like a…cat."

The girl looked at the kittens that were scampering about the floor. There must've been at least six, but even Thomas could tell from the look in the little one's eyes that she knew and loved them all.

"Does she have a kitty already?"

Thomas solemnly shook his head. Cilla edged closer to him. He restrained himself from putting a supporting hand on her shoulder.

Following a sigh, Joanne reached out and pulled a passing kitten into her arms. "Then you need this one." Her chin quivered. "My *schweschdere* will understand." After giving the kitten a brief hug, she scrambled nimbly to her feet and handed the young cat to Cilla. Cuddling the kitten to her chest, Cilla smiled at the little girl. "Thank you."

Thomas nodded at Joanne. "She'll give it a *gut* home." He turned to Cilla. "And that's where we need to be heading. I have work to do."

He returned to the parlor as the two girls waved goodbye. Thomas didn't recall exactly how many, but the Zooks had several children. Maybe some Visiting Sunday, he could bring Cilla over. He'd enjoy a *gut* chat with Isaiah, and Cilla could play.

"I imagine you have ample hay and grain, but probably not something to feed this size and species yet." Isaiah grinned as he handed Thomas a small bag with a double-fisted amount of cat food inside. "*Gut* luck on your expanded herd."

Thomas tipped his hat down to cover his reddening face as he followed Cilla and the mewling kitten out of the parlor. "*Denki*. I'll need it."

Fortunately, the kitten didn't try to leave Cilla's lap on the trip home, although it did express its concern at its new circumstances during the journey. It almost made Thomas wish for a return of the silence, but, glancing over to see Cilla's glowing face, he knew he didn't.

"I'm going to name her Flower."

He stifled a snort at the name. "Flower?"

"Yeah. It goes with Bambi and Faline. It's the name of the skunk in the movie."

Thomas's eyes rested on the little black-and-white kitten. Why anyone would want to name anything after a skunk was beyond him. The kitten finally settled down. With it, silence settled over the buggy. And for once, it didn't roar.

It'd begun to rain after they got home with the kitten. To Thomas's relief, Cilla seemed content to stay home that day instead of running off to Emma's. She played in the barn, entertained between the cat and the calf. He knew, because he'd checked on her a few times.

His business kept him busy enough, but that day he didn't have any pressing work. Although it was a nice break, it was also a potential problem. Maybe the boys had been right to leave for other opportunities. There was enough work for one blacksmith in the district, but maybe not enough for two or more. He missed them. He missed working with them in the shop. His youngest, Noah, had been particularly talented before he'd left to join his brothers in Shipshe. Thomas muttered when his hammer slipped and wrinkled the strip of metal he was working on. Blacksmithing was hard, solitary work. *Ja*, they'd been right to leave. Lost in his thoughts, he looked up with a start when Cilla poked her head into the shop.

"I'm going over to tell Emma about Flower." She was almost all the way out the door before she reluctantly returned at his bellow.

"Nee!" Her face fell at his decisive response. Her jaw firmed. Her eyes narrowed. Thomas sighed. One step forward. Two steps back. It had been raining all day. The creek would be up. Maybe not that much, but enough to make the rock crossing questionable.

"I think I have a dish that I need to return to her. If you'll give me a moment to finish this, I'll hook up the buggy and we'll drive over." He watched as her jaw softened and eyes lit up. They stayed that way even when he added, "But the cat stays here."

"Would the dish be the one that's sitting on the counter? I'll get it." And she was gone again.

Thomas's lips curved slightly as the door banged shut. He could get the hang of this connection thing. If only it didn't mean all these trips to see Emma.

Emma glanced out the kitchen window at the sound of a buggy coming up the lane. It'd been a busy day. The rain had kept folks out of the field and sent them shopping. But whenever she'd had a free moment, she'd look in the direction of the woods, worried that Cilla might try to cross the creek in these soggy conditions.

At the sight of Thomas's rig, she raised her eyebrows. Going to the door, she opened it in time to see Cilla scramble down from the buggy and dash up on the porch. The casserole dish and cover she carried rattled precariously.

"We got a kitty like Willow!"

Emma almost dropped the glass in her hand from a combination of shock and fleeting weakness from arthritis. Hastily, she set it on the nearby counter. Her gaze bounced from Thomas's staid expression to Cilla's exuberant one. "You did?"

"Yeah! From a farm with a lot of cows. I named it Flower. I wanted to bring her over, but he wouldn't let me. He said we shouldn't because we didn't know how the cats would get along."

Emma's surprised gaze settled on Thomas. Flushing under her regard, he scowled. She suppressed a smile. "Well, he's probably right."

"We've set up a spot for Flower in the barn. Safe and secure."

"That sounds like a *gut* plan." The smile was getting more difficult to control.

Cilla set the empty casserole dish on the counter. Taking an exaggerated sniff, she bent and looked into the oven window. "Otherwise he's been okay today, but he's a terrible cook. So can we stay for supper?"

Chapter Four

Thomas's blue eyes widened at Cilla's pronouncement. Obviously, he hadn't been party to the dinner request. In fact, from the look on his face, Emma figured it was probably best he not eat anything too soon, as he'd probably choke on it.

Although his apparent discomfort tempted her to smile, it also stung. Even before she'd been in his company as Priscilla's best friend, she'd been around him and his family as a neighbor. They hadn't been close, not like she'd once dreamed they would be, but they'd been at ease with each other. When it was obvious which way the wind was blowing on his interest, she'd been very careful to tamp down her own feelings. So what had she ever done to make him so clearly uncomfortable with her?

Emma's gaze shifted from Thomas's unsettled expression to Cilla's eager one. Whatever she responded, someone was going to be unhappy. Between her two potential guests, that outcome would be the least change to Thomas's normal demeanor.

"So he hasn't improved in the kitchen then?"

Cilla's brow drew down. "Improved? I don't think it's possible that he could be any worse."

"Oh, anything's possible. And I suppose it's more than possible that the casserole will stretch to feed three." Emma pulled out a drawer to retrieve some pot holders. "You've just enough time to wash your hands. Then you can help set the table."

Smiling brightly, Cilla promptly disappeared to the bathroom to do as instructed. Thomas's expression wasn't nearly as cheery.

"If it's an inconvenience, we can go." His voice was as stiff as his posture.

"Thomas." Emma propped her hands on her hips as she faced him. "Over the years, I've had numerous meals at your house and you've had plenty at mine. What's one more?" For a moment, she thought he was going to respond. But after giving her a hooded perusal, he pivoted and headed down the hall from where Cilla was returning.

Cilla pulled plates from the cupboard Emma had wordlessly pointed out and carried them to the table. "Didn't you say you had a sister? The one who baked the cookies? Why isn't she ever here?"

Emma grinned as she set the steaming casserole on a hot pad. "Makes you wonder if I made her up, does it? Elizabeth works at a restaurant in town, the Dew Drop. Her hours can vary. You just happen to be here when she isn't. But I'm sure you'll meet her sometime. She's like me, only different."

"Is it nice having a sister?"

In the process of cutting bread, Emma paused with her knife halfway through the loaf. Watching Cilla studiously organize the cutlery on the table, her heart clenched at the girl's wistful tone. "*Ja. Ja*, it is. Surprisingly, even though Elizabeth and I are twins, we weren't always as close as your *grossmammi* and I were though. Sometimes you choose friends who'll become as close or even closer than family."

Cilla's head remained down, her attention on Emma's resale shop china plates. "If I could choose my family, I'd choose you."

Emma blinked rapidly against the instant threat of tears. *Ah, Cilla. Priscilla would've loved you so. And you her.* A movement from the corner of her eye had her glancing toward the hallway beyond the table. At Thomas's set expression, Emma ached for the both of them. Briskly, she finished slicing and carried a plate of bread over to the table. "Pick me out like you did your kitten, would you?"

To Emma's relief, Cilla allowed the conversation change as they all sat down and gave a silent prayer. "I didn't actually pick her out. The little girl, Joanne, decided which one to give me."

The skin on Emma's forearm prickled to see Thomas's blacksmith-muscled one resting next to it on the table on her right side. Her table had never felt so small. She tried to recall if she'd ever eaten with him in the absence of Priscilla. Realizing this was the first time, she cleared her throat as she struggled to remember the gist of the conversation. "Do you like your kitten? Flower, *ja*?"

"Oh, yeah! She's perfect."

"Then maybe Joanne knew which one would best suit you, and that's why she gave you that particular one." At the accidental bump of Thomas's rock-solid leg under her small table, Emma found herself babbling. "Amish communities sometimes have women who serve as matchmakers. They determine men and women who might best suit and get them together."

The news obviously intrigued Cilla as much as accidentally sharing it dismayed Emma.

"Really? That sounds like a cool job." Reddening under the girl's considering gaze, Emma scrambled for another topic before the question arose as to whether she'd ever used one. Or worse, why was she still single if something like that was available.

"Perhaps, as your *grossdaddi*'s cooking hasn't improved, maybe you'd like to learn how and take over in the kitchen."

Cilla's eyes rounded. "I'd like that." She grinned at her grandfather. "And for sure and certain, it couldn't be any worse."

Emma laughed at Cilla's use of the common Amish phrase.

Even Thomas's lips twitched. "For sure and certain, indeed," he murmured over a mouthful of casserole.

To Emma's relief, for the rest of the meal she and Cilla discussed plans for Cilla to start cooking. Thomas's contributions were limited to a few grunts, interspersed with a few grimaces. Emma tamped down pride that he'd eaten several servings and had all but licked his plate clean. Probably more a reflection of their limited culinary options at his house than of her cooking skills, but still, his obvious enjoyment of the food pleased her.

After supper, Cilla, unprompted, began helping with the dishes. For some reason, Thomas made Emma nervous, sitting there at the table watching them work. She shooed him into the living room, where he sat down and picked up a newspaper off the nearby end table.

"Where do these go?" Cilla gestured with the quart jar she held up by way of stuffing her hand, dishtowel included, inside it.

"They go back down to the basement with the rest of the vegetable jars. There's a shelf for the empty ones."

Cilla went to the door Emma indicated and opened it. Upon looking at the wooden stairs that disappeared into the darkness, she shut it again. "It's dark down there."

Emma smiled. It was indeed. It didn't bother her now, but when she was young, she'd detested being tasked with transporting jars to or from a basement that was inhabited by crickets, spiders and an occasional mouse. "You don't have to take them down. I'll get them later."

"No. It's all right. It'll be an adventure. But I sure miss electricity and being able to flip on a light switch." Readily taking the flashlight Emma pulled from a drawer, Cilla opened the door and flicked on the beam. Jars rattled in her arms as she cautiously descended the stairs.

"The empty jars go on the back wall. Do you see them?" Remembering her own trepidation as a girl, Emma hovered at the top of the stairs.

"*Ja.*"

Emma smiled at the Amish word that floated up the stairway. The beam of light flipped around in the basement as Cilla shifted it to put the jars on the shelf.

A moment later, her young voice drifted up again. "Wow, you have like a grocery store full of jars down here. So many! And…like a wooden box of potatoes. And onions! What're in the bags hanging on the end of the shelves?"

"Shine the light on them so I can see." The beam steadied on lumpy, loosely woven sacks suspended by nails along some of the shelves. "Oh, those? Those are husked walnuts."

"They don't look like walnuts. They're dark brown, round and wooden-y looking."

The girl's experience with walnuts was apparently limited to what was in a store or a cookie. "They need to be shelled."

"Why aren't they? Is that something we can do?"

Emma grimaced, unconsciously stroking the stiff joints in her fingers. Normally she loved the winter evening activity of cracking the shells—the nutty smell it released, the flash of satisfaction at freeing a perfectly formed nut-meat kernel from inside the seed. But shortly after she'd obtained the many bags below, the ache in her fingers had become too much to ignore. The prospect of applying the needed pressure to the hand tool in order to crack the shells made her wince.

Elizabeth, never one to keep her opinions to herself, loved to bake with walnuts, and usually was impatient to have some available by the Christmas season. But this year she hadn't said a word about the nuts still hanging in the sacks in the basement rather than shelled in the cupboard. Nor had she suggested they get to work on them in the evenings. Although she didn't mention it, Emma figured her sister had noticed the issues she'd been having with her hands.

Her shoulders rose in a heavy sigh. Cilla sounded so excited. She didn't want to disappoint her. And Elizabeth would be happy to have at least some of the nuts made available. "Do you think you can handle bringing up a bag?"

"Sure!" The girl's enthusiastic response was followed by a clatter, signaling a bag had been tugged from a nail and dropped to the floor. With another sigh, Emma strode into the living room to collect newspapers to put under the upcoming project. As she was gathering a few outdated ones, she glanced over to meet Thomas's considering gaze. Furrowing her brow at his intent look—he was looking at her like she hadn't lived next door all her life—

Emma straightened abruptly and retreated to the table with several newspapers tucked under her elbow. Struggling over harvesting the walnuts in the kitchen would be preferable to trying to decipher the tough nut to crack in her living room.

Thomas frowned. Emma's hands were bothering her. Having already read these editions of *The Budget* and *The Connection* at home, Thomas had used the Amish newspapers more as a camouflage to watch the pair in the kitchen than to actually read the news. He'd had to remind himself to turn a page occasionally just to keep up the pretense.

When Lena—he caught himself and shook his head—Cilla had invited themselves to stay for supper, he'd been aghast. Following four years of practice in avoiding Emma, his recent awareness of her was...new and strange. An additional reason to avoid her. He'd loved his wife, loved her still. Any awareness of another woman seemed...disloyal. But supper had been nice. Hearing their soft-spoken conversation flow about him had been pleasant. After so much time spent alone, it was surprising the comfort that arose from watching and being part of their bustling activity. Particularly that of the little brown wren.

While she'd agreed to his granddaughter's request to extract the walnuts, it'd been with much more reluctance than enthusiasm. His gaze above the drooping newspaper rested on Emma's hands as she efficiently spread papers over the kitchen table. Thomas stroked his beard as he recalled Emma's *mamm*. Even as a boy, he'd recognized that his neighbor had struggled with her hands. Before he'd realized it, Thomas was setting down the paper he wasn't reading and pushing to his feet. As he strolled into the kitchen, Emma dubiously watched him approach.

"I assume you're ready to go. Cilla will be disappointed, but this is something she and I can do another time."

"*Nee*, I came to help."

Emma looked at him like he'd just declared that he'd decided to close his smithy to open a quilt shop. "Help? With the walnuts?"

"Well, I was never much of a hand with dishes. I think I waited long enough that they're already done. Besides, you said I needed to connect with her. Sitting around a table cracking nuts would be pretty connecting, wouldn't it?" He lifted an eyebrow. "As I'm already here, I don't have to report that I'm making an effort to do so, right?"

Was that a blush blooming on her cheeks?

How interesting. Emma was rarely unsettled. Thomas rubbed a hand over his mouth to hide his smile.

Emma dropped her gaze to the newspaper she was unfolding. "I supposed the first thing would be getting them up the stairs. Cilla might need your help. The bags can be a bit heavy."

With a nod, Thomas headed down the wooden steps. He found Cilla and her unwieldy burden on the fourth step from the bottom. Relieving the girl of the bag, Thomas threw it over his shoulder with a rattle of nuts.

Cilla preceded him up the stairway at an eager trot. "I've never done this before so I don't know how."

"*Ach*, we have. I suppose between us, you'll get a good lesson."

When he entered the kitchen, a few bowls had been added to the paper-covered table. A wastebasket, presumably to collect the shells, was tucked underneath it. Thomas swung the bag from his shoulder. At a nod from Emma, he untied the string at its top and scattered a number of the brown nuts onto the table. Leaning the still full bag against a table leg, he settled into the chair next to it.

"Cracking walnuts takes as much patience as anything else."

Cilla frowned at Emma's comment. "Then

I'm in trouble, because I'm not very good at that." Fingering a walnut, she plopped down in her own seat.

"I think you'll find you'll have as much patience as you need." Emma set silvery tools on the table. Two had two slender lengths of metal roughly five inches long, hinged at the top. Along the upper inside, the metal was ridged with teeth to hold the nut. Thomas picked one up and turned it in his hand, wrinkling his nose at the flimsy apparatus. In his shop, he could easily make something two or three times this sturdy for the task.

Cilla rolled the walnut in her hand. "They look like they're made of tree bark."

Emma smiled. "They look even different when they're on the trees. A green hull covers these shells that needs to be removed first. These were husked and dried last fall. It takes a bit of effort to get down to the nut, but it's worth it. Especially when they end up in Elizabeth's cookies."

Wedging a walnut at the hinged end of a nutcracker, Emma's hand closed around the opposite ends. If Thomas hadn't been watching her face, he wouldn't have seen her fleeting wince as she tightened her grip. With a self-conscious laugh, she wrapped her other hand around the first and applied pressure until a quiet crack erupted and a few pieces of the shell tumbled to the table. When she set down the small handheld vise, another momentary grimace crossed her face as she stretched out her hand.

Thomas had seen enough. "I'll do the cracking. You two use those—" he nodded to the slender metal picks with sharp pointed ends "—to get out the nuts. Even two against one, I believe I'll still stay ahead of you."

With one of the picks, Emma deftly freed a section of nutmeat. She gave Cilla an exaggerated, wide-eyed look. "Did he just challenge us? We'll have to make him eat his words." When Thomas snagged the nutmeat from the table and popped it into his mouth, she gave his hand a tart pat. "And not the fruits of our labors."

Years of hard work in his shop had made Thomas believe the skin on his hands was as tough as the thick leather gloves he occasionally wore. And that he was immune to any scorching, as he frequently worked with heated items. But where Emma had patted him felt like a cinder had popped out of his forge and landed on the back of his hand. His fist tightened around the nutcracker. The walnut wedged in the device's teeth shot out to bounce over the table and skid across the linoleum floor. Willow, who'd sauntered into the kitchen to investigate all the activity, bounded after it, batting it with her paws.

Emma smiled at the cat's antics. "I'm surprised she made the effort. She usually considers herself above playing."

Cilla giggled as she bounced a walnut in her hand. "Do you think Flower would like to play with these?"

Emma picked out another nutmeat. "I'm sure she would. Take a few home with you. If Willow, with her more mature years, finds them entertaining, your kitten will have a delightful time."

Thomas wasn't feeling very mature himself. Cracking walnuts here at the table was surprisingly as entertaining to him as chasing one across the floor was to the cat. He couldn't recall ever shelling them with Priscilla. So there were no memories to face. There was simply enjoyment in the unexpected activity.

Cilla and Emma laughingly encouraged one another as they tried to keep up with him. When they struggled, they alternatively moaned or facetiously complained that he was cheating by barely breaking the shell, leaving them to do all the work with their slender picks. When Cilla reached across the table for a fractured shell, he snatched a nut from her bowl.

"Hey!" She pointed at him.

Mockingly, he lowered his brows and glowered at her. Unintimidated, she pitched a shell fragment at him. When it stuck in his beard, Thomas crossed his eyes and looked down at it. Cilla dissolved into a fit of giggles.

Glancing up, he caught Emma smiling at him. Her eyes were warm with laughter and... approval? Was that twinkling he saw in their brown depths? For a moment, Thomas forgot to exhale. No one had twinkled their eyes at him in so long, he wasn't sure. The sight gave him an odd fluttering in the stomach. Maybe he'd eaten too much tonight. *Ja*, that had to be it. The definite improvement from his own cooking had made him overeat. And the unexpected evening had been more than pleasant. That was why he was feeling odd, an unaccustomed mixture that fluctuated between unsettled and...content.

Thomas kept a surreptitious eye on Emma as they worked their way through the bag. His reasoning was to ensure that picking the nutmeats from the shells didn't bother her hands as much as cracking them obviously had. It certainly wasn't because the lamplight made her look serene and pretty.

Pretty? The walnut wedged in the nutcracker shattered into a plethora of pieces that scattered over the newspaper. Darting a questioning glance at him, Emma quickly picked out a section of nut that might be salvageable and swept the rest of the fractured pieces into the wastebasket.

His lips pressed into a flat line, Thomas retrieved another nut. Efficient. Emma was so efficient. That's what he was admiring. And if picking out the nuts was painful, her face didn't reveal it. He narrowed his eyes as the tool in his hand wobbled under his grip. Still, he could make her a better nutcracker in his shop. One that could do the work without having to apply hand pressure. It wouldn't take him any time at all. In fact, he had a piece of walnut leftover from a long-ago project that would make a nice base. He'd bring it over next time he came. When he'd been young and new at the trade, he'd made several little gifts for Priscilla while they'd been courting.

The nut he was squeezing slipped. Thomas barely withheld a yelp as he pinched his finger in the device's ridged surface. Courting! Where had that crazy thought come from? He wasn't going to be doing any courting. Dropping the nutcracker, he shoved his chair back from the table.

Emma and Cilla looked over in surprise at the ensuing screech against the linoleum. Thomas pushed to his feet. "Bag's empty. Time we went home."

Brushing walnut shell fragments from her apron, Emma rose from the table as well. "*Denki* for all the help. I can't believe we've finished that much already."

"Can we do it again sometime?" Cilla selected a nut from her bowl and nibbled on it.

Emma glanced at Thomas and apparently read the scowl on his face. "I don't know. It's up to your *grossdaddi*."

Thomas's gaze bounced about the too-comforting kitchen, skipping past the too-tempting woman to land on his granddaughter's hopeful face. "We'll see. I've got work to do at home."

"When are you going to teach me to cook?"

Although her attention stayed on Thomas, Emma gave Cilla a small smile. "We'll see," she echoed him.

Thomas gave her a short nod for not countering him. Emma had always had good sense. It was him who wasn't showing rationality now. Determining he'd wait outside for his granddaughter to say her goodbyes, he swung open the front door and strode down the porch steps. Courting! Of all the foolish things to pop into his head.

Chapter Five

Head tilted toward the woods, Emma absently pulled the last towel from the clothesline and folded it. Was that laughter? Her lips tipped in a smile. The sound was one that hadn't come from the direction of Thomas's farm in a long time.

Since the unexpectedly pleasant evening cracking nuts, she hadn't seen Cilla. But the young girl—and her grandfather—were never far from her mind. Several times in the past few days, her gaze wandered toward the woods that separated their properties. As Cilla was apparently staying home, Emma hoped that things were going well between the pair. From the muffled laughter that filtered through the burgeoning trees, obviously something was. She was glad. It was a *gut* step for both of them. Although Emma missed the girl's company. And her grandfather's.

Smoothing the towel so intently she was creasing the folds, Emma strove to bring her mind to order as well. *Stop thinking of him. Ja,* it'd been pleasant to have Thomas share the evening with her. Something he hadn't done, willing or not, since Priscilla was alive. *Ja,* he might've paid particular attention to her, more than he ever had before. Attention that sparked the stubborn ember, that'd always resided in her heart for the man, to flare to life. She'd spent the past few days tamping it down. She knew better than to lower the walls guarding her affection for Thomas. For him, there would only be one woman that he'd ever love. Priscilla. Always Priscilla. It would be so much easier if Emma hadn't understood his loyalty.

Adding the towel to the neat stacks already loaded in the laundry basket, she hefted the wicker carrier and propped it on her hip. The faint laughter floated to her again, ousting her troubled musings with its joyfulness. Intent on its unseen origin, Emma drifted to the back step, where she set the basket down just inside the mudroom door. With only a moment's hesitation, she let the door swing shut and headed toward the woods. And the beckoning laughter.

Following it through the trees and budding underbrush, she found its source. Cilla's skills with her hair and *kapp* had definitely improved. Still, the *kapp* flopped on its perch as the girl bounced along the far bank of the creek. Emma was glad the normally intrepid girl hadn't tried to cross the nearby rocks that provided a precarious passage. Today, the creek level was high enough that crossing, while possible, would be risky.

"What are you doing?"

Cilla glanced up at Emma's call and grinned. "I'm chasing frogs. I've never done it before." She scrunched up her nose. "There weren't any where we lived in town. At least I couldn't see them. And I didn't know what they sounded like until Grandpa told me what the funny noise was the other day."

"Catch any?"

"Yeah. But I don't have any pockets to put them in, so I let them go again."

Emma smothered a smile. Although she knew some women who sewed them in at the waistband, pockets weren't an acceptable part of their dresses in their *Ordnung*. Probably a *gut* thing in this situation. "Sounds like a reasonable plan."

"Do you want to help?"

Emma laughed. "*Nee*. I'm quite comfortable accepting that my days of chasing frogs have passed."

Cilla squatted to swish her hands in the

creek, rinsing off some of the mud that dappled her arms up past her wrists. The effort was admirable. But as mud also coated her shoes, streaked up her spindly legs and dragged down the bottom of her dress with its weight, it was like brushing teeth while munching cookies—unproductive. Emma bit the inside of her cheek, making a mental note to check if the expanded Reihl household needed help with laundry.

When Priscilla had passed, Emma had offered to do laundry in addition to occasionally bringing over meals. Thomas had adamantly declined. She hadn't persisted. It was one thing to put a casserole dish in the man's refrigerator. It was something else entirely to fish his clothes from the washer and hang them on the line. Thomas, more than most men, liked his privacy. He'd seemed to be holding his own alone. But—eyeing the girl's mud-spattered garments, a smile stretched across Emma's face—Thomas wasn't alone anymore.

Cilla propped her hands on nonexistent hips. "How about racing sticks down the creek like you said you used to do with my grandma? Are you too old for that?"

Too old? The term gave Emma a twinge. Besides, she recognized the girl's desire for a playmate. Even an *old* one. Scanning the surrounding area, she selected a likely-looking candidate and strode to the creek's edge on her side.

"I should say not." She accepted the challenge. Her fingers rubbed along the smooth wood. *I hope I don't regret this.*

Giggling in delight, Cilla rapidly chose her own short stick. By tacit agreement, they dropped their contestants simultaneously from the opposite sides of the stream. Emma, having played in the creek extensively when she was young, released hers directly into the current. The small piece of wood immediately skipped along downstream. Cilla huffed in frustration when hers meandered along the bank.

"Retrieve it and drop it into the faster moving water."

With a quick nod, Cilla heeded Emma's advice and snatched the listless stick to pitch it farther into the creek where the water rippled. Emma had moved only a few steps downstream when she froze. She watched the girl darting along the opposite bank with narrowed eyes. Without thinking, she'd spoken in *Deitsch*. And Cilla had unerringly responded. Which meant...

"I'm falling behind!" Cilla moaned as her stick hung up on a rock.

"I doubt that," Emma murmured. Lena had

obviously taught the girl. Why would Cilla pretend not to understand the community's language when she apparently did? What other secrets did she have?

"You're too slow," Cilla hollered from across the creek when her stick swept off the rock and shot downstream.

"I'm beginning to wonder that myself."

Ducking under branches and weaving in and out of the brush that fringed the creek, they followed and cheered on their racers. Sometimes one would be ahead. Sometimes the other. Sometimes the sticks were almost out of sight around a curve before they caught up through the tangle of undergrowth. They were about even when Emma's stick caught in an eddy some distance downstream from where they'd started.

"How far do we go?"

Emma leaned out with a longer branch to poke her contender into faster moving water. "We can go all the way to the bridge in this direction. Upstream is a different story. It gets pretty boggy up that way, and if you aren't careful, you'll quickly discover what you think is solid ground, isn't."

"Um…you mean like this?"

Emma glanced over to see Cilla windmilling her arms in an effort to remain upright. Her shoes had disappeared in gray-black mud that clasped above her slender calves. Emma's eyes widened. A small sluggish waterway seeped over the shallow bank into the creek. The area surrounding it held water like a sponge. The girl had bounded straight into the mire.

"Oh, dear. *Ja.* But even much worse. Can you get out?"

Cilla flexed one knee, then the other, struggling to free herself from the possessive muck. Her hands fluttered as she teetered alarmingly.

"Uh, I don't think so. And my stick is getting away."

"I'm thinking we'll call the game a draw while we work out your situation." Worrying her lip, Emma gauged the possibility of Cilla extricating herself and her own ability to safely cross this area of the creek. How far around the girl's location did the treacherous ground extend? Would she get stuck in a worse position trying to cross here? Brow furrowed, she glanced upstream toward the rocks.

"Can you stay upright long enough for me to get over on your side?"

"Probably." Cilla's arms shot out as she wobbled again. "If you hurry."

Emma hurried. As she did, she reassured herself that, even if Cilla pitched into the creek, although cold and wet, she could at least push her head above the water until Emma could reach her. Still, not a comforting thought. So she ran, ducked and dodged the branches and shrubs that reached out to snag her skirt until she reached the rock-strewn passage.

Panting, she rested a hand on her stomach as she considered them. She'd once known every secure foot placement on their slippery surfaces, but she hadn't crossed them in a long time. Years. And as creeks do, the capricious nature of the water had repositioned the rocks during that time.

"Are you coming!" Even the faintness of the call couldn't diminish the urgency in Cilla's voice.

Hissing in a breath, Emma jumped over an expanse of water to skid onto the first rock. Maintaining a three-point touch—two feet and one hand always in contact with rough surfaces—she scrambled over the makeshift bridge. On the last speckled granite stone, her foot slipped off to splash into the water. Gasping at the cold dunking, she leaped the remaining short distance to the bank.

Squishing with every other step, she dashed down Cilla's side of the creek. While her pace slowed, her breathing didn't when she finally emerged from the brush to find the girl still upright.

Feet planted facing the creek, Cilla swiveled at the waist as far as she could toward Emma's direction. Her eyes were wide. "I'm truly stuck."

Emma leaned against a bough to catch her breath as she studied the situation. "I would say so." Spying a likely-looking branch, she retrieved it from the underbrush. Edging as close to Cilla as she dared, she extended one end to her. "Can you grab this?"

Cilla twisted, grimaced and twisted some more. "I'll try." Missing on the first swipe, she snagged the branch on her second sweeping grasp. The momentum sent her swaying. Struggling to stay upright, she lunged backward with a hard jerk on the branch. On the other end of the limb, and the tug, Emma jolted forward.

Cold clamminess slid over her foot to grasp her ankle. With a startled squeak, she tried to wrench free of the sludge. Wavering between laughter or tears at their predicament, she landed on the side of laughter. At her snickering, the stricken look dissipated from Cilla face and she giggled as well.

"*Ach*, I just failed in my rescue."

"Well, at least the stick helps me keep my balance. As long as you don't let go."

"If I sacrifice my shoe, I might be able to get my foot back out to dry, or at least drier, land." Shifting her weight to her back leg, Emma tried to wiggle her foot to loosen it from the now concealed shoe. Feeling it slip free, she jiggled harder. As her stockinged foot emerged from the muck, her planted foot slid from the solid ground down into it. Tipped backward with both feet too far under her, she lurched onto her bottom in the chilly mud.

Her scrabbling hands jerked the stick, tugging Cilla toward her. With a loud shriek, the girl landed on her side in the mire, sending a tsunami of the slop to splatter over Emma from her chin down to her shoeless foot.

"Are you all right?" She immediately reached toward Cilla.

"Yeah. But I think my grandpa's going to be upset with me."

The old Thomas under Priscilla's influence, probably not, but the Thomas of the last four years, possibly. He'd become a stick-in-the-mud. Emma began to chuckle. "We'll worry about that later. Right now, we still need to get you—make that us—free of the muck."

Interspersed with laughter, they maneuvered to do so. By the time they extricated themselves, both were slathered with the odorous sludge. Thrilled to have finally escaped the mud's clutches, they crawled to sit, slightly panting, on questionably solid ground a few feet back from its edge.

Emma's stomach ached, but it was a good hurt. She hadn't laughed so much in far too long. The laughter seemed to do Cilla good as well. Her face, what could be seen of it behind the mud, was glowing. Following Emma's lead, she'd been grinning throughout their blundering adventure.

That alone made up for Emma's current miserable condition. Her own face was growing stiff where splattered mud had begun to dry. When she wrinkled it at the malodorous smell that coated her, flakes caked off from the end of it. With a further grimace, she huffed the crumbled sediment away from her lips. Wrapping her arms around her bent legs, she shivered in her clammy dress at the bite of the cold wind that now blew down the creek. They needed to get home and clean up, but she was oddly reluctant to break the comradery of the afternoon when Cilla had so obviously enjoyed it.

A twig snapped behind her. Emma stiffened. Probably a squirrel. Scampering through the carpeting leaves from last fall, they were the loudest things in the woods. Whatever it was, it made too much noise for a deer. Or a bear. Sightings of those were rare, but they were occasionally seen in the area.

"We look like swamp creatures."

Although she smiled at Cilla's comment, Emma cocked her head to concentrate on her hearing. Bears stuck to more remote areas. Or so she hoped. Emma frowned at her fanciful thinking. A bear? Extremely doubtful. Besides, even a hungry one would probably think twice before dining on anything that was as coated with muck as they were. Had to be a squirrel. Or maybe a deer that decided, with their noisy laughter, that it was too crowded on this section of the creek. Still, as Emma rubbed a hand over the gooseflesh that dotted her arm along with the mud, she couldn't shake the feeling they were being watched.

Thomas's urgent pace slowed when it became obvious the voices he heard over the quiet murmur of the stream weren't in distress. Halting his mad dash, he sucked in a few deep inhalations to steady his breathing. Hopefully his heart rate would soon follow suit. It'd leaped into a runaway pace the moment he'd stepped from the barn to hear a shriek carried on the wind.

Knowing Cilla wasn't in the barn, he'd glanced at the house. But she wouldn't be there either. Although she'd thankfully kept close to the farm in the past few days, she rarely stayed inside. He did a quick scan for any sign of her amidst the outbuildings. A farm was a dangerous place. An unsuspecting person, and that defined his plucky *kinskind*, could get hurt in many ways. Leaving the barn's Dutch door creaking on its hinges behind him, he vaulted the fence to the pasture and descended the hill with long strides.

His few attempts at calling were futile; the wind blew the sound right back up the hill. Thomas saved his breath to race toward the creek, pausing every several paces to listen. Which direction had the scream come from? Sound was distorted in the woods. Uncertain where to start, he'd headed for the rocks where she'd been known to cross.

He took his first real breaths when he found two sets of footprints in the soft soil along the creek's edge, heading downstream. At least she wasn't alone. Working his way along the bank, he caught fragments of animated voices. He'd been slapped and thwacked by every piece of underbrush in the woods before he recognized the animation as merriment, not fear.

His heart rate slowing to something resembling normality, Thomas leaned against a bud-laden tree to listen. There'd been laughter surrounding the table at Emma's home a few days ago. His pulse hiccuped at the memory of the unexpected enjoyment in her company before he guiltily steadied it. But he hadn't heard outright hilarity for some time. Or if he had, he'd avoided being around it. This exhilaration, with the calming quiet babble of the stream a few yards beyond him, began to unravel the edges of an unrealized knot that had taken residence in his gut.

The lower-pitched, still obviously feminine chuckle, he didn't recognize. The sound reminded him of Emma's subtle laughter the other evening. Lifting his hat, Thomas ran a hand through his hair. What was with him lately? It might be spring, but he didn't need to be acting like some young fool with stars where his eyes should be and hankerings for courting turning his brain to mush. Courting. There was that word again. He tugged the hat back down over his forehead. He'd do better keeping his heart and mind encased in perennial winter. A barren winter since Priscilla had died.

Where had she found this playmate? It seemed to be one who was good for her. The higher-pitched laughter was his granddaughter. Another burst of laughter erupted from the unseen pair. Thomas couldn't stop the upward twitch of his mouth at the sound. Just because his granddaughter was enjoying herself didn't mean that *his* life had to change. In fact, it was *gut* she was discovering there was joy in Amish life as well as rules and expectations. She'd surely discover even more pleasure when she went to live with one of his sons, where they'd have a normal family situation instead of residing with the grumpy old man he knew he'd become. His smile wilted. The prospect of her leaving didn't bring the enthusiasm it had when he'd first considered it.

Ach, enjoying the sound of laughter after years of self-imposed solemnity didn't mean he had to join in. But he was sorely tempted when he pushed off the tree and wove his way between the draping branches and underbrush to see the source. When he finally caught sight of the pair, he rubbed his hand over his mouth to wipe off a surprisingly wide smile. He'd seen pigs in a wallow that were cleaner.

Churned-up muck told the tale of how the two ended up on the ground, slathered in greenish black from their foreheads to their feet. The tail end of a shoestring amid the viscous sludge was the only clue of what might've happened to their shoes.

Thomas didn't recognize the other female. She was about the same height as his granddaughter and petite in build. Her *kapp*, still surprisingly white, was more secured than Cilla's, but even it was tipped off the back of her head to expose neatly contained mink-brown hair that was mostly spared from the mud.

Thomas's eyebrows rose at the sight of the dark hair. Visions of it loose had plagued him since seeing it. As had his churning thoughts regarding the woman whose hair it was. The corners of his lips lifted until his eyes crinkled. He was safe. This caked-with-mud woman, so far from his sweet and proper Priscilla, couldn't possibly be a threat to his peace of mind.

Chapter Six

❧

"I guess I'll have to put more water in the horse trough to get all that washed off you two."

Both of them spun at his words. Emma struggled to get upright. Thomas tucked his chin to hide his smile when, after a bit of scrambling in her mud-covered stockings, she slid back down.

"But I'm afraid if you wash off in there, the horses won't ever drink from it again. Come on. Let's get you cleaned up and see if it's really my *kinskind* and neighbor under all that sludge."

His granddaughter struggled upright. She eyed him warily, as if expecting him to toss her back into the bog. "You're really not going to yell at us?"

Thomas winced inwardly at her expectation. A previously realistic expectation. He drew a lengthy inhalation. "Can't. I'm all out of breath from running down the hill to conduct a rescue when I thought I heard a scream."

A smile creasing her face, his granddaughter skidded over to him on her shoeless feet. Grabbing his arm, she left a muddy handprint on the fabric. "Thanks, *Daddi*."

Knees nearly buckling at the shortened version of the term for grandfather, Thomas almost slipped to the ground himself.

With a low chuckle, Emma plucked at the clammy clothes that clung to her. "*Ach*, I suppose I'm not opposed to a rescue."

Her wry amusement and laughing eyes sent a ripple up Thomas's spine, over his broad shoulders and down to his fingertips. His breathlessness returned. The urge to haul her diminutive figure up from the ground and into his arms startled him. Startled and disturbed. Startled and deluged him with guilt. Clenching his hands, Thomas momentarily closed his eyes to block out the captivating sight of her.

How could he ache to respond to Emma's smile when Priscilla was the best wife and helpmate a man could've ever asked for? Although she was gone, he still felt married, still felt the need to be loyal to her. Bishop Weaver had come out to visit him a few years ago to talk about remarrying. Thomas hadn't been rude, but the bishop hadn't bothered him about it since. He knew other widowed men in the district remarried, some with considerable haste, but he couldn't betray Priscilla that way. It would be like leaving her behind. Like moving forward without her. His throat rippled in a hard swallow. He couldn't do that.

But he also couldn't leave Emma sitting on the chilly ground.

With a contradictory blend of reluctance and longing, he extended a hand. Following a slight hesitation, she took it. Instead of sensing the cold mud that oozed from between her fingers, Thomas absorbed the warmth and fragility of her hands. He kept his grip gentle, remembering her joint soreness and knowing that, after years of wielding a hammer, he could easily crush hers.

With that same strength, he pulled her toward him. Due to the vitality of her personality, he'd expected more resistance, more weight, only to find her light as a feather. With a hissing inhale, he locked his arm at the last moment to prevent her from colliding with his chest. Not because he was leery of the muck clinging to her. But because he was fearful he'd be the one to cling, once she was tucked against his chest. Tucked against his heart, where no woman but Priscilla had ever been.

Emma wobbled at her abrupt halt. Thomas fractionally tightened his hand to steady her. She barely reached his shoulder. Her eyes, those laughing eyes, looked up at him from a mud-dotted face.

He wasn't aware of lifting his hand to wipe the worst of it away with a gentle thumb until she went still at his touch. Her smile faded as their eyes locked.

Thomas had known Priscilla was the one for him since he'd first seen her in school decades ago. Since then, he'd never been tempted by another woman. Until now. He yearned to kiss the lips that'd somehow escaped the splattering. The hand clasping hers pulled her closer. His thumb brushed faintly over her cheek as he lowered his head. Emma's eyes widened as her mouth parted.

"Brrr. With that wind, I'm freezing in these wet, gross clothes."

Thomas didn't feel the wind at all. He definitely didn't feel the cold. But he jerked back at Cilla's words. Emma trembled before him. It was hard to tell who dropped whose hand the quickest.

Kneeling, ostensibly to wash the mud from his hand in the creek, Thomas drew in ragged breaths. *He'd almost kissed another woman.* What was the matter with him? First courting had popped into his head and now kissing. Gnawing his lip, he struggled to harness his renegade emotions. *Priscilla. I'm sorry. It'd been so easy for years to stay faithful to you and now... I don't know what's come over me. But I don't like it.*

The chilly water numbed his fingers. As the overnight temperatures still dipped below freezing this time of year, he wasn't surprised. Not a *gut* place for the women to wash off, but maybe a *gut* one for him to plunge into head-long to jolt him from his foolishness.

The stockinged feet next to him fidgeted from one leg to the other under a mud-laden hem. If the water was that cold, what coated them wasn't a far distance behind. Even as he watched, Emma shivered.

She had to be miserable. Later, he'd get himself in hand, but right now, he needed to complete his rescue, such as it was. His place was closer than Emma's, and on this side of the creek. It surely wasn't neighborly to pull an unsuspecting woman into his arms and kiss her. But it also wouldn't be neighborly to expect her to traipse all the way to her pristine house when his *kinskind* was responsible for the woman's current condition.

Rising to his feet, Thomas cleared his throat.

"No point in messing up your place. Might as well come over and wash up in mine."

He flicked a glance toward Emma. She was going to decline. He could see it on her face. It was a *gut* thing. Still, he stifled his unexpected regret with what he told himself was a relieved sigh.

"Oh, please come over! You could help me make something like we talked about at your place. Otherwise we'll just have sandwiches. Again. I used to like peanut butter and marshmallow creme, but we've had that so much lately, I can hardly choke it down." Cilla finished her plea with dramatized gagging.

Thomas was pretty tired of church spread himself. "I've got some eggs. And a bit of bacon. I could fry them while you two are cleaning up."

"As long as he doesn't try to fix potatoes at the same time, it shouldn't be too awful. Please say you'll come."

Emma was quaking in earnest now. Frowning, Thomas placed a light hand on her shoulder and directed her toward a path away from the boggy area. "While you're deciding, let's at least get moving."

She shuffled ahead of him. "I have no clothes. It would be foolish just to put this," she picked at her dank apron, "back on again."

"I'll find you a dress to wear." Cilla dodged under a branch. Her muddy attire and shoeless state didn't slow her down.

Thomas pursed his lips, impressed at the girl's solution. Lena had left dresses behind when she'd joined the *Englisch*. Priscilla had kept their *dochter's* clothes, unable to let them go in her hopes and prayers that someday she'd return. He'd understood. He'd kept all of Priscilla's things when she'd died. He just wasn't… ready to part with them.

When Cilla had arrived to his stunned surprise, he'd moved her into Lena's old room. Once he'd told her the clothes in the dresser had been her *mamm*'s, she'd been willing to wear them. After a bit of experimentation with pins, Cilla had figured out how to make them fit. He eyed the woman trudging ahead of him. With Emma's tiny build, anything that would work for Cilla would work for her as well.

"Sounds like it's settled." Thomas guided them out of the woods and through the pasture fence. The sun dipped toward the horizon beyond the hill as Cilla dashed ahead. Thomas kept behind Emma, blocking the breeze from her as much as possible. His steps slowed when he realized what he was doing. Sheltering Priscilla while they'd been courting had made him feel strong and protective. He needn't shelter

Emma. They were only neighbors. Not a courting couple. He was never going to be part of
a couple again. He'd had a wife, the only one
he ever needed. He dropped farther behind.
The women were already inside by the time
he reached the house.

Emma wondered how clean Cilla actually
was, the girl having been through the bathroom before she'd even peeled her soiled stockings off in the mudroom. For the first time
ever, she felt awkward in her neighbor's house.
Felt awkward using the shower Thomas had
put in for Priscilla years ago. Awkward de-
scribed the whole evening thus far. She'd even
felt awkward the moment Thomas had arrived
at the creek to witness her filthy appearance.

When he'd offered his hand, she'd almost re-
fused it. What woman wants to feel mud ooz-
ing between her fingers the first time she takes
the hand she'd always dreamed of holding? Not
that she'd thought of taking his hand for over
half a lifetime. But there'd been that moment
when he'd pulled her up. She'd almost thought
he'd meant to… She shook her head. *Oh, how
foolish, Emma. He wasn't going to kiss you.
The reason he was looking at you so intently
was because he was wondering how a woman
could get so dirty.*

Filthier than she'd ever recalled being. Perhaps, although it was awkward, Thomas was right. It was preferable to have all the mess in one household. She'd come over and do this laundry for him at least. Emma poked the sodden pile with her toe. Half of it was hers, after all.

As promised, Cilla had left clothes. Hopefully everything Emma needed. Maybe she should've seen to that herself before cleaning up, but she hadn't wanted to trail mud through the house in her search. She eyed the stack on the small vanity.

Her breath caught at the splash of apricot material on the bottom of the pile. Carefully, she moved the other articles to reveal the dress. Running a finger over the fabric, Emma swallowed. They'd been shopping together when Priscilla had found the fabric. Emma had squashed her envy that she couldn't find a color that did for her what the apricot did for Priscilla. It'd brought out the strawberry highlights in her hair. It'd made her skin glow. They'd cut out the material for the pattern together, giggling as they did so in anticipation of an upcoming social. Emma had seen her wear the dress a number of times. Had noticed the admiring gazes that'd trailed after Priscilla on those occasions.

Other than the blue one she'd made for her wedding and had been buried in, this had always been Priscilla's favorite dress.

Inhaling deeply, Emma almost caught the scent of the soap her friend had used. She took a step back. *Nee*, she couldn't wear this. Putting it on would be difficult, much too difficult. Not that the dress would be uncomfortable, but wearing the memories would be.

Tiptoeing to the door, she listened, hoping to hear Cilla within quiet hailing distance. It was silent beyond the door. Emma considered opening it a crack and calling, but, frowning, she quickly dismissed that. It would be too embarrassing if Thomas was within earshot.

Returning to the soggy pile on the floor, she stooped to pick up her own dress. Shuddering at the thought of putting it back on, she dropped it with a wet *thwack* back onto the heap. *Ach*, she'd put Priscilla's dress on, go straight home and change. She couldn't stay here wearing it. She'd be distressed and Thomas surely more so. With compressed lips and a prickling at the backs of her eyes, Emma slowly dressed.

Thomas lowered the heat a fraction. This time, he wasn't going to burn them. Jimmying the spatula under one of the eggs, he pried it from the bottom of the skillet. Not burn all of them, at least.

Emma should be out soon. Cilla was humming as she set the table. Sprinkling salt over the eggs, he winced as more poured out than expected. *Ach*, it was so much easier to cook for one. No expectations. No pressure. Hopefully the women would be hungry enough, they wouldn't mind the taste. After all, this was just a neighborly gesture, nothing more. Wasn't it? Then why was he nervous?

He and Cilla both looked up at the sound of a door opening. Tentative footsteps came down the hallway. Thomas's lips quirked as he wondered about Emma's hesitation. Had Cilla not brought pins along with a dress? His pulse kicked up a notch. Had she not been able to contain all that lustrous hair?

When Emma appeared from the hallway and edged uncertainly toward the front door, his face froze, along with the rest of him. It seemed impossible that he could lift an arm to point at her with a shaking finger.

"Where did you get that dress?"

Their eyes wide, both Emma and Cilla flinched at his tone.

There was a clatter as Cilla dropped silverware onto the table. "I got it for her. I found it in a dresser drawer in one of the bedrooms."

Thomas knew which one. The bedroom he'd moved out of as soon as the funeral was over. Not able to stay in that room with its lifetime of memories—their wedding night, the birth of their children, her loss—he'd taken up residence in one of the other rooms. In what used to be their master bedroom, he'd removed all his possessions, but he'd left other things, her things, just as they were before.

He even knew which drawer the dress had been in. Its color had always reminded him of Priscilla's hair. Hair that was tucked up away from everyone else, only to be let down for him. When he saw the dress, he'd always thought of Priscilla's hair. Now when he thought of the dress, his first thought would be of how well Emma, with her tidy figure and rich brown hair, looked in it today. His stomach churned. Beads of sweat dotted his forehead. Another memory replaced.

"You had no right." His voice shook as much as his pointing finger.

"I'm—I'm sorry. I know it was my grandmother's. Everyone always talks about her, and so I thought…"

"You had no right," he repeated, hardly able to get past the thickness at the back of his throat. Cilla's shoulders stiffened under his glare.

"And you." Thomas jabbed his finger at

Emma before dropping his hand to his side. "I don't care how you try to charm me. Cook my food. Clean my house. Even going as far as to dress in my wife's clothes. You're not going to take her place."

Guilt added an extra edge to his voice as he knew, over the past few days, he'd been imagining having Emma in his life in just that manner.

Emma's face above the bright apricot was white. "I know I could never take her place." Her voice was barely a whisper. Without another word, she slipped out the door, shutting it with a sharp click behind her.

The two remaining in the room stared after her before Cilla whirled to face him. "How could you! You mean old man. I hate you!" A moment later, another door shut, this time with a slam. In the moments that followed, the silence roared like never before.

Chapter Seven

Thomas drew in a slow breath. At the burned smell that assaulted him, he numbly turned and flicked off the gas stove under the charred remains of the eggs. Slowly, shakily, he made his way into the living room. Easing his way into his chair, he felt like a man twice his age.

How could he? The words echoed in his head. He could, because he was afraid. Afraid of a longing he was struggling to deny. Closing his eyes, he dropped his head into his hands. *Priscilla, it was said in loyalty to you.* But his wife would've been unhappy with the way he'd done it. Disappointed in the way he'd acted. And toward her best friend no less. In her gentle manner, Priscilla would've chewed him out. Not by raising her voice, but by shaking her head in that sorrowful way and quietly reminding him that he was better than that.

Thomas scrubbed his hands over his face. Everything was so muddled. He was suddenly living with a granddaughter he hadn't known existed. Doing the best he could in the situation, but it would've been so much better if Priscilla was alive. She'd have known what to do and would've done acres better than his fumbling.

But Cilla's arrival wasn't the only thing creating turmoil. He'd comfortably loved one woman all his life. Been loyal to one woman. Now... Now he had feelings for another. *He* was far from thrilled about that.

Lifting his head, Thomas slumped back in the chair. Priscilla would've been more upset over the way he'd just treated Emma than that he was...interested in her friend. In fact, she'd have been glad about the possibility. His fingers curled around the ends of the wooden armrests. Glad for both of them. Hadn't she said toward the end, "I know you, Thomas, know what you're inclined to do. When you're ready, Emma's a *gut* neighbor. A *gut* woman. Keep your eyes and heart open."

He frowned. What if she hadn't meant his natural inclination to reject Emma's overtures to provide some meals for him? To clean the house? To perform other household tasks Priscilla had known he'd omit? What if she'd actually meant... Had his wife given him her blessing to marry her best friend? Priscilla had certainly been capable of thinking ahead that way. Thomas's stomach suddenly hollowed in a strange way. And if so, was he ready to seriously consider the possibility?

A muffled thud sounded from down the hall. Like something had been knocked to the floor. Thomas ran a hand through his beard. And in all this tumult, had his *Englisch*-raised grandchild just berated him in the Amish dialect?

The girl wanted to know about her *grossmammi*. It was understandable. Lena might've shared some things about her *mamm*. He shouldn't be hoarding happy memories of his life with Priscilla, like a miser hiding his wealth away in a dark and secure place.

He and Emma both had myriad memories to share. It would be nice to talk about the *gut* times with her. *Ach*, Emma. She had never tried to charm him as he'd just accused her. It was he who'd unwittingly wanted to change the situation. And had taken his guilty feelings out on her. Closing his eyes, Thomas rubbed his forehead. He owed her an apology—*if* he ever got brave enough to face her again. In fact, he should go over and do it now.

His eyes shot open. When she'd walked out the door, he'd been consumed with his guilt and consternation. He hadn't thought a whit about Emma. How was she getting home? Surely she wouldn't try crossing the rocks after dark? But not crossing them left her with a long walk on a cold night.

Lurching to his feet, Thomas jerked open the door and rushed onto the porch. Though he scanned the yard and the nearby road, there was no sign of anyone in the dwindling twilight. Returning to the house, he grabbed his hat from the nearby peg and headed for the barn. He'd harness Banner. Surely they could catch up with her and take her home.

His steps slowed. He'd known Emma all her life. She was like a radish—sometimes mild and sometimes unexpectedly hot. He'd hurt her. That hurt would migrate to anger. Even if he did catch up, she might refuse to talk to him and keep walking anyway. Still, he had to try. Turning at the barn door, he looked back toward the house where a dim light glowed in Cilla's window. Thomas sighed as his hands rested on the latch. He needed to tell his granddaughter he was going out. She probably wouldn't talk to him either.

Grimacing, he retraced his steps to the house. *Ah, Priscilla. Life without you is so complicated.*

Emma's pace finally slowed from the almost run that'd taken her down Thomas's lane. She swiped her hand against her cheek, dashing away a tear. A tear of what? Embarrassment? Certainly. Anger? She'd get there. Rejection? At the word, her eyes stung again, threatening a deluge.

She'd been rejected. Her stomach twisted, threatening to have her retch on the side of the road. In her hidden longings, rejection was a possibility. But as long as nothing was spoken, it wasn't…final. Now it was. It struck at her deepest fear—that she wasn't enough as she was. Always a leftover. Not a blessing. Now, not even a second choice. She hitched in a breath as a few more tears leaked from her eyes.

Although she and her sister had been twins, Elizabeth was a pound bigger at birth, a size differential that'd continued all their lives. So as they were growing up, while Elizabeth received new clothes, Emma always had hand-me-downs. Her first new dress had been one she'd sewn herself. When she and Priscilla ran together, Emma always felt like a dull shadow next to her lovely and charming friend, but it didn't matter because she loved her so. A life of being perennially second was why she'd become a hatmaker. Besides providing an income, joy filled her at seeing customers, particularly children, receive something new. It was likely her hats were later handed down, but it wasn't something she witnessed.

Emma rubbed her hands over the sleeves of her arms. At least her embarrassment was helping keep her warm. If she'd thought about it, she would've grabbed a rug from the buggy. But all she'd thought about was getting away. Disappearing from his sight before she could embarrass herself further by bursting into tears, or worse…begging him to see her differently.

She sniffed. At least she was dry. Although, given the situation, she'd rather have been cold in her own clammy dress. Emma picked at the apricot fabric under her fingers. She felt counterfeit in its bright color. A color Priscilla had worn like the ray of sunshine she was. But as Thomas had rightly pointed out, she wasn't Priscilla. He didn't even want her as a replacement. She'd been kidding herself. She'd known her walls were crumbling. Under the onslaught of feelings for Cilla on top of the long-buried ones for Thomas, she hadn't shored them up. Had she said something, done something that let her buried feelings show because she'd foolishly started to believe something was possible between them?

Well, she'd learned her lesson tonight.

Thomas wasn't interested in any relationship

with her. That didn't mean he wouldn't, at some point, be interested in someone else. Priscilla had asked her to watch out for Thomas after she was gone. Emma had done her best. She'd kept her ear to the ground for any romances or unions of convenience that might include his name. When they'd figured enough time had passed after Priscilla died, some of the bolder widows and single women had come sniffing around Thomas. Emma couldn't blame them. Although they were small, his farm and business were successful enough. He was a hard worker and a physically attractive man, and he would perhaps someday again find joy in the world. But he'd never gone looking for a wife. She watched him at the meals after church. He'd never seemed partial to any particular woman when they were serving and had congregated with the men as soon as possible.

She wanted him to be happy. But Emma knew in her heart that, although she didn't want him to continue in his current loneliness, it'd be hard to see him with someone other than Priscilla. Would she ever get over "why not me?"

Why not her? The bishop sometimes put pressure on widowed folks in the district to remarry. Emma twisted her lips. What did that say about her and Elizabeth that Bishop Weaver

didn't seem to be interested in seeing them settled with husbands? Did he think they were already settled pretty well, with Emma making
the community's hats and Elizabeth's skills in
Miller's Creek's restaurant giving it a reputa-
tion that drew folks in? As single women, they
could have a job outside the home. But if they
were married, the rules were different.

Although twilight was fading, the rising
moon lit the road ahead of her bare feet. An owl
called from the nearby woods. Emma found a
sliver of peace at the sound. She sighed. *For
I have learned, in whatsoever state I am in,
therewith to be content.* Ah, maybe in time
she'd find contentment again, as the *Biewel*
said. Contentment without Thomas, as she had
for years until recently.

But did that mean she needed to be content
without anyone? Or that she should cast her
attention elsewhere? Who knew why she'd always longed for Thomas? *Gott* had just shown
her that door was closed. Perhaps it was time
to open another. Perhaps she needed to show
Thomas she wasn't chasing after him by being
involved with someone else. Emma twisted her
lips. Was it more to show Thomas, or herself?
Did it matter as long as she found someone?
Her pace surged again as she resolved to do so.

The distant sound of water cascading from

the culverts indicated she was getting close to the bridge. The journey by road had gone faster than she'd figured. Easy to do when her pace was fueled by emotion.

For a brief moment, she'd been tempted to take the shortcut. But the rocks had been treacherous even during daylight today. It would've been beyond foolishness to try crossing them in the dark. Besides, as her hand slid down the cool fabric of her skirt, she knew she couldn't risk getting Priscilla's dress torn or dirty. She needed to wash and return it as soon as possible—just not when Thomas was there.

The water rumbled under her feet as she stepped onto the bridge. In the distance through the trees, she could see the lamplight in her window. Elizabeth was home, probably wondering where Emma was. When she'd followed the sound of the laughter to the creek, she'd never envisioned the laughter would, for her, turn to heartache.

At the sound of hoofbeats behind her on the road, Emma hurried up her lane. She knew it was Thomas. She couldn't face him. Not now. Not for a while. Her face burned again at the memory of his rejection. She couldn't bear to see the look in his eyes again when he saw her in the dress. Tomorrow, she'd visit Susannah Weaver, the local matchmaker. It was past time to turn firmly in another direction and do it quickly before she lost her nerve.

Content in all things. *Ach*, she'd failed in that. Because of the many things she was feeling, contentment wasn't among them.

Emma patted her cheeks to relieve some of their flushed heat. With a final swallow and useless hope that she didn't look as embarrassed as she felt, she tentatively tapped on the screen door. When there was no response after a few seemingly endless moments, her ensuing sigh was a blend of relief and disappointment. Turning from the door, she jumped at the sight of Susannah Weaver coming up the porch stairs. The possibility of backing out of the mission had just diminished.

Susannah's smile was bright in a face already tanning from time in the sun. "Sorry to startle you, Emma." Her brow furrowed. "Is everything all right?"

"*Ja*. Everything, well, most everything, is fine." Emma shifted her feet. Heat climbed back into her cheeks. Although she looked with longing toward her buggy, she recalled last evening's humiliation, dismay and loneliness that'd driven her to see the matchmaker. With a fortifying breath, she followed Susannah's brisk stride into the kitchen.

"I've been out preparing the barn for the service this Sunday. Can I get you anything to eat? Or some coffee? Or tea?"

Automatically shaking her head at the offer, as Susannah's lack of skills in the kitchen were well-known in the community, Emma paused. Having something to hold on to as she stumbled through her request would be helpful. "*Kaffi* would be nice."

"That I can handle." Susannah nodded to the table for Emma to take a seat as she set about making some. "Always a pleasure to see you. But—" she cast a shrewd glance at Emma over her shoulder "—I'm guessing there's a particular purpose for this visit?"

Emma sat, immediately knitting her fingers together. She massaged some of her stiffer finger joints in the ensuing silence. "I…um…"

She took a hasty sip from the cup Susannah set down before her. A long exhale cooled her mouth from the hot drink and helped frame her thoughts. It'd been easier practicing on the way over this morning than facing the sympathetic gaze of the recently happily remarried widow.

"Remember when we were cleaning at the house Hannah and Gabe Bartel bought before they moved in? You'd just made a match for Naomi and Leroy Albrecht? And…um… I asked if you knew of anyone for me?" Emma clenched the cup so tightly she was surprised the crockery didn't shatter. "Well, I was wondering if...you had yet." Finishing in a rush, she forced herself to look up from the dark brew that threatened to splash from the cup in her trembling hands.

"That was a fluke." Susannah gave her a self-deprecating smile.

"Ja." Emma winced at memories of the previous night and the lonely walk home. "But I'd rather take a chance on your fluke than no chance at all."

The empathy in Susannah's gaze almost made her tear up. When the woman reached a hand across the table, Emma pried one from her cup to reluctantly grasp it. The comfort generating from Susannah's compassionate squeeze rippled up Emma's arm to relieve some of the tension in her chest.

"I don't know why the men of Miller's Creek haven't realized what a treasure you are. Honestly—" Susannah's lips twitched "—with Jethro off the market, I can't think of any off the top of my head who would do you justice."

Smiling ruefully, Emma withdrew her hand to resume her stranglehold on the cup. "I'd settle for someone from the far reaches of your memory at this point."

Resting her elbow on the table, Susannah

propped her cheek on her palm as she considered the white painted ceiling.

"Well, I wonder if Thomas Reihl is ready to consider marriage again."

"Nee." Emma's cup jerked, splashing coffee on the table. Susannah's eyebrows rose briefly as she regarded Emma's flushed face. Without a word, she rose to retrieve a dishcloth to wipe up the spill.

"You're probably right. But perhaps some time. The addition of an unexpected granddaughter might change his plans."

Emma squirmed on the hard kitchen chair. "Whether they change or not, he isn't one I'd be interested in."

Having returned the dishcloth to the sink, Susannah sat again. "I can understand that. Thomas has become quite the grouch lately. I hope his granddaughter doesn't decide he's too difficult to live with."

Emma frowned. That wasn't really fair. *Ja*, Thomas could be a bit grumpy. But he had every reason to be. Even after all this time, he was still missing Priscilla, his sons had moved away so he had no one to leave his business to and he'd just found out about Lena's passing. She leaned forward. "Oh, he's very *gut* with Cilla. I think he'll be even better as they get more adjusted to each other."

The corners of Susannah's lips twitched. There was a curious light in her eyes as she slowly nodded. "If you say so. Still, sounds like he's one to keep off the list."

Folding her hands in her lap, Emma pressed her lips together. Her shoulders drooped. "*Ja.* I'd say so."

"Hmm." Susannah went back to perusing the ceiling. "I heard Henry Troyer was thinking about remarrying. As a newly-chosen minister, he might be shifting to actively pursuing the possibility."

Emma pressed the more troublesome of her finger joints against the cup's comforting heat. Henry Troyer? He'd been widowed for less time than Thomas had. She'd known his wife. But thoughts of marrying Henry didn't trouble her like the thought of replacing Priscilla in Thomas's life did.

"Do you think he'd want to pursue in…my direction?"

"He would if he was wise." Susannah smiled. "And he strikes me as a fairly wise man. Particularly if he knew there'd be a possibility of a welcome reception."

"Would he be concerned that at my age the time may have passed for giving him any more children?" Emma's eyes widened slightly when Susannah flushed and touched a hand to her stomach. Pregnancy wasn't something spoken about in their culture. Was the remarried widow expecting? If so, although Susannah had older children, it would be a first for her husband, Jethro. Emma sent up a quick prayer for the couple, who'd both had heartache in that area during their previous relationships.

Returning her hand to the table, Susannah cleared her throat. "Henry already has several adult children. Although some men do, I don't see him as one to seek a new wife for that purpose."

Emma was surprised at the tightening in her stomach and the sweating of her palms now that a defined candidate might make her distant dreams a possibility. "What do I do? I haven't walked out with someone in years. And even then, I apparently didn't do it very well, because here we are. Do they still call it 'walking out' at my age?"

Susannah grinned. "I don't know. Maybe by our age we can call it ambling, or maybe strolling out."

"Strolling. I like the sound of that." Emma understood why the reluctant matchmaker was considered so good in the role. She was wonderful at getting folks to relax.

"Even though Jethro and I were faking our courtship, at least at first, I was still so nervous when we'd be seen together. I felt like everyone was staring at us."

Pressing her lips together, Emma relived her embarrassment at Thomas's accusation that she was throwing herself at him. "Maybe that's something I need. For folks to know I'm seeing someone." At least for a certain someone to know. To see that she was interested in someone else and not him. After a while, she might even believe it herself.

"I'm still unsure of this unexpected role of matchmaker, but if you think my help would find you someone you'd be happy with, I'll gladly be involved. Shall I visit Henry and see if he's interested in stopping by for a hat…or something else?"

Emma felt like she was on the edge of a precipice. If something came of it, the action would change her life. Was she ready for that? Would she always wonder and regret what might have been possible if she backed away now?

"Or something else." Her breath hissed out in a combination of apprehension and relief.

"And I'll do some more thinking. See who else I can come up with. I might have to go a little farther out, but I'm sure there are many men who'd be happy to have you as a *fraa*. This role might be new for me, but I have a feeling there's a definite someone for you."

They both looked toward the open window at the clatter of hooves coming up the lane. Emma rose to her feet, torn between a sigh at ending this surprisingly comfortable chat with Susannah and a grimace at being caught by someone at the matchmaker's home. Of course she could say she was just visiting, which they had been. Visiting about finding a man for her after all these years. Emma was comforted that, though new in this role she may be, Susannah had always been discreet.

When the new arrival appeared in the doorway, Emma smiled. For whatever reason the young woman was visiting, it wasn't about needing a matchmaker. Sarah Raber was this generation's version of Priscilla. Lovely both inside and out, she surely had the young men lining up to walk out with her.

Opening the door, Susannah gestured the dark-haired girl inside. "Rebecca's finishing chores in the barn, Sarah. You can join her there, or she should be coming in soon."

"Here is fine. The *kaffi* looks *gut*."

"What are you girls planning this morning?"

Sarah smiled charmingly. "We thought we'd do a little fishing."

"Fishing? With worms and everything? That doesn't sound like my daughter. Unless—" Susannah pursed her lips "—there's a young man involved."

Sarah's smile grew until a dimple creased her cheek. "Well, actually, Rebecca overheard while she was waitressing that a few of the guys were going fishing this morning. She stopped over last night on her way home from work and asked if I'd join her. She didn't want to go alone."

"I should hope not." Susannah shook her head.

"Oh, she's not that bad. There's one she's hoping will ask to take her home after a Sunday night singing. She thinks he just needs a little nudge." At Susannah's dubious expression, Sarah added, "I'll be a *gut* friend and not tell who it is."

"Is there someone on this 'fishing' trip whom you're interested in?" Susannah set a cup down in front of the young woman.

"Nee." Sarah wrinkled her nose.

Emma was glad to be talking about someone else's situation. What would it be like to be on the other side of the fence? Where you didn't go looking for men, but they came looking for you? "I would imagine several are interested in you. That's got to be…exciting."

"I suppose." The young woman shrugged.

Emma frowned. "You don't sound enthused."

The corner of Sarah's mouth tilted in a half smile. "It's sometimes hard to tell who's really interested and who just wants to win the competition. I have *breider*. I hear them talk. Fellows, or at least ones my age, are interested in what someone else has. If someone gets a fast horse, everyone wants a faster horse. If someone gets a new, improved plow, everyone wants a new plow." She sighed. "Sometimes I feel like some are interested in me just because others are. I just want one special someone."

Emma had never considered there was such a thing as having too many beau.

"Maybe, in that way, it's good to be thrown into Gideon's company. I know where I stand. He's a friend. One who's not interested in me that way."

Susannah raised her eyebrows. "Gideon Schrock? Now, he's one I've had a number of mamas ask to set up with their daughters."

"Maybe that's one reason we understand each other. All the rest of the girls seem to flutter around him. I wish someone would make enough progress that they'd go walking out. It seems every wedding we attend, the bride pairs us together as *newehockers*."

Emma smile was subdued. She'd been a side sitter at a few weddings. No matter whom the bride tried to pair her up with, the young man hadn't been interested enough to pursue anything further. Emma couldn't even remember whom Priscilla had set her up with for her wedding. Her emotions had been so chaotic that day; giddy with happiness for the new bride and a guilty melancholy for unrealized dreams.

"Well, are you going to find someone for Gideon then?" Sarah grinned, the dimples making another appearance.

"*Nee*, I think Gideon is capable of making his own plans. When someone is, I don't bother their process. I just try to help folks see things that they might not have realized themselves."

"I'm afraid I sound more flippant than I am. It's just that… What is the saying? It's hard to see the trees for the forest? I'm afraid in the midst of the forest that I'll miss my special someone." The girl's blue eyes were solemn. "Maybe it's *gut* then that I'm always thrown together with Gideon. At least our constant pairing slows things down."

Emma smiled wryly. "I haven't even seen a tree for several decades. I wouldn't mind walking through the forest for once." She caught Susannah's considering gaze. The intent attention made her flush. Rising to her feet, she carried her cup to the counter. "And speaking of walking, I need to get going. The shop might not be open, as it's Thursday, but I still have several things to do." Her smile wavered slightly as she turned to her host. "*Denki* for the *kaffi*. I understand if…nothing comes of what we spoke about."

"I'll see what I can do." Susannah smiled impishly. "I think you'll be surprised at the outcome."

Chapter Eight

Even in the silence Thomas couldn't hear himself think. Not that he wanted to. Because when he did, he relived Emma quietly walking out the door. As he lined the metal over his anvil, his stomach clenched at the memory, just as it had when Emma stepped into the room last night. His first thought had been how lovely she looked. That impression had withered like dry paper set to flame when he'd realized she had on Priscilla's dress. Memories of the many times he'd seen Priscilla wear it had flooded him. How he missed her, how he longed for just one more time to walk into the kitchen and see her there, donned in that dress.

And how guilt had swamped him, as he'd been visualizing another woman in his wife's kitchen up until that moment.

Now he knew Priscilla would understand.

Had understood, had even quietly encouraged him to look in Emma's direction. Did that make him feel better? Thomas brought the hammer down with more force than necessary. Maybe. Some. But the belatedly recognized encouragement to see his neighbor in a different light wouldn't help if Emma never talked to him again.

Heat rose up his neck, not from the fire in the smithy, but at the memory of his harsh words and actions. Emma hadn't been trying to get his attention; he'd been flattering himself. That any woman would want his attention, the way he'd been acting, would be a shock. No wonder she'd preferred a long, cold, dark walk instead of his company for a ride home.

He'd never caught up with her. Thomas brought the hammer down again. Although a relief at the time, he should've checked on her, made sure she got home all right. She was too wise to try the rocks at night, wasn't she? *Ja*, she was. Emma had a lot of common sense; she wouldn't do anything foolish. But then, he always thought he had common sense as well. And look at him now. He was a mess—undone by a child and a lifelong neighbor.

A child who hadn't talked with him since last night. Cilla had no reason to know how the sight of Priscilla's dress on someone else would affect him. His shoulders slumped at the way he'd snapped at her. And they'd been getting along all right before that, or so it had seemed.

Of course, maybe he was a poor judge of his relationship with young ones, as all his children had left home. Because of him? Thomas swallowed against the bile threatening the back of his throat. He'd always wondered. Lena had gone when she'd been a teenager, the boys, as soon as they'd reached their maturity. He'd hoped his youngest would stay, as he'd be the one who'd inherit the farm, but Noah had followed his *breider* to Indiana. Were they leaving for opportunities, like they'd said, or just leaving? He stared unseeing at his anvil. Maybe he shouldn't even wait to hear back from his married sons about taking Cilla. Maybe he should just take her down to them on the bus himself, before she, too, left on her own.

He hadn't been his best since Priscilla died. Thomas snorted at the understatement as he raised the hammer again. No point wishing he could go back and handle it differently now. Now was the time to make amends, starting with the girl currently in his household. Laying the hammer down, he strode to the door of the smithy.

Where was she? There'd been no response last night when he'd knocked on her door to inform her he was going out. Finding no solace in sleep, he'd risen early this morning to go to his shop before chores, as hammering on things had seemed like a *gut* idea in his current mood.

Thomas rubbed a hand down his face. What if she'd gone to Emma's? That would be a just punishment—to have to face them both at the same time. Cilla, so full of energy, had been expending it by ignoring him. Hopefully he'd find her in the barn. The cat, whatever its name was, was there, but he'd turned the Jersey cow and calf out into one of the pastures. The previous few days, it seemed if she wasn't with one, she was with the other.

He ran his fingers over his beard. Maybe he left her alone too much. How long could one kitten entertain a girl? Was loneliness why Cilla was so prone to taking off? All the more reason for her to join his sons in Indiana.

Please don't make me go over to Emma's. I'm too embarrassed to do so.

Coward. The word rang in his ears as loudly as his hammer did against the anvil. Afraid to face one pint-size female he'd known all his life. Turning back to the shop, Thomas banked his fire. He'd stop at the pump, get a drink and check to see if Cilla was in the house. If she wasn't, he'd check the barn. If not there—Thomas sighed out what felt like a week's worth of air—he'd head for Emma's by way of the creek.

To his dismay, the barn, like the house, was quiet. All but the Standardbred were out in the pasture. Thomas checked the hayloft before he found the kitten sleeping, curled up in one of the empty stalls. It opened its eyes when he approached, but closed them again, recognizing he wasn't a playmate. So where was she?

Exiting the barn, Thomas looked out over the pasture toward the creek. Removing his hat, he scrubbed his fingers through his hair. Where else could she be but Emma's? *Ach*, hopefully her anger didn't burn so bright that she stayed there until after dark. As long as she was home before dark, he'd let her come back on her own time. If the sun went down and she still wasn't home... Well, he'd have to face Emma whether he was ready to or not. In the meantime, he'd work. And fret.

Jerking his hat back down, Thomas paused when he noticed one of the Belgians in the pasture with his head up, looking not toward Thomas at the barn, but toward the creek. Striding toward the fence, he climbed up on the first rail and looked down the hill. Two more of the big chestnut draft horses had their heads up, their attention directed at the creek.

Thomas's jaw clenched in irritation. Surely she hadn't gone down to the creek again? He hadn't told her not to, but couldn't she learn anything from the incident yesterday? Still, his pulse sped up, as this section of the creek was where the skeleton had been discovered years ago. He'd built a fence to keep the livestock away, but the barrier hadn't stopped Cilla yet.

Clearing the fence, Thomas headed across the pasture at a half jog. The horses glanced in his direction before looking back down the hill. As he approached the first gelding, Thomas jerked to a halt. He froze as he searched for the source of the faint call. Had he heard something? Or was it his imagination?

There it was again.

"Cilla!" He jolted forward a few steps, afraid to go too far in case he lost the sound in the wind.

"Help!"

This time there was no denying the cry. Thomas ran downhill toward the sound, his head swiveling to locate its source. The Jersey cow was crowding the wooden fence at the bottom of the hill. Her chest strained against the top railing. Her tail lifted in agitation. No calf was at her side. Thomas lengthened his stride.

"Cilla, where are you!"

"We're here!"

And then he saw them.

The pair was almost hidden amongst taller tufts of earth, crowned with early spring vegetation. The path to them was a churned mixture of green and greasy black, revealing the ground surrounding the tufts looked solid, but wasn't. A scarf dangled off the back of Cilla's strawberry blond hair. Her blue dress, what he could see of it, was coated with mud. She was up to her slender hips in the green-tinted slime.

"Grandpa! I can't get him out!"

Cilla's hands were propped under the calf's head. The fawn-colored muzzle barely cleared the surface of the muck. The little one's legs were buried. White ringed the distressed wide brown eyes. Mud splattered the tawny coat over his heaving ribs. The youngster was exhausted. Even as Thomas scanned for a possible approach, it let out a pitiful bawl, one immediately answered by his anxious mama.

Thomas's mouth went dry as he did a quick survey. He wasn't going to be able to get to them, not without sinking in himself. They were too far into the muck. If he got stuck, no one would know where they were. Or where to begin looking. His racing pulse throbbed through his clenched hands.

The calf bawled again, too weak to even

struggle. A good thing, as doing so would only work it deeper into the slop. As much regret as he felt toward the little Jersey, he couldn't worry about it. He'd be lucky to rescue one. It wouldn't be the calf.

Cilla's teeth were chattering. How long had she been encased in the chilly muck? His stomach churned at the possibility that she might've been calling for hours while he'd been fretting about apologies.

The calf's head sagged. Grimacing, Cilla leaned closer to keep its flaring nostrils out of the mud. She shot a beseeching glance at Thomas, her eyes almost as wide as the frantic calf's.

Arms spread wide, Thomas cast about for something, anything, to get to them. The only thing he had right now to reach over the distance was his voice.

"I'd have thought you had enough of the mud yesterday."

"I thought I did too. Until I came out to see Bambi. And saw that he was stuck." Her voice was hoarse, but steady.

Thomas spied a branch lying under the draping limbs of a tree. Racing over, he tugged it free of the underbrush and dragged it back. Bracing it with one hand and guiding it with the other, he stretched it out to her.

"Grab hold of it!"

Staring at the lifeline with longing, Cilla shook her head. "I'm not going to let go of him."

He shook the branch. "Grab it!"

"No. I'm not going without Bambi. He needs my help. We have to get him out first."

"I can't get you both out." It was said through teeth gritted in fear. "Grab it. You'll have to leave the calf."

Cilla's chin trembled as she again shook her head. "I'm not leaving him. I won't go without him."

Ach! First Emma walking home last night in the dark and now Cilla refusing to leave the calf so he could save her. Why were the females in his life so stubborn?

Tossing the branch to the side, Thomas took a step toward the girl and calf. His foot immediately disappeared up to the ankle. Leaning back, he wrenched it free and shook off the muck. Rubbing a hand over his mouth, he glared at the pair.

"You're shivering. I need to get you out."

"He's cold too, and he's just a baby. I'm afraid you won't get him if you get me first."

She was right. Hands braced on his hips, Thomas's breath came out in a gust. "I'll be back as fast as I can."

The distressed cow's attention was so fixed she didn't even flinch when Thomas vaulted the fence beside her. He ran up the hill, spooking the Belgians who trotted away, their short tails lifted. For half a stride, he debated grabbing a collar and line to pull the pair out. He rejected it, as even his most stable draft horse had his neck arched and was snorting through his huge nostrils at the unexpected commotion.

Thomas knew he could catch the gelding, knew even in the horse's agitated state that the big animal would obey his commands. Still, one stride by the horse might be too much and dislocate one of his granddaughter's joints by pulling too fast from the sucking mud. The calf was probably too far gone anyway, but there wasn't getting one without the other.

Bursting into the barn, he skidded on the straw-strewn floor and wheeled toward the area where he kept his tools. Reaching it, he flung open the door. Hands on both sides of the doorway, he breathed in bellows as he scanned the wall. There it was. Thomas lunged across the room. The come-along winch clattered against itself as he jerked it from the wall. On the way out the door, he grabbed a length of rope from a nearby nail.

The ratcheting tool was useful for many things, from delivering a calf to stretching wire to build a fence. Today, he was depending on its small incremental movements to pull a child from danger. Thomas ran back across the pasture, the tool slamming against his leg at every jarring downhill stride. His heart clenched as he caught sight of them.

"Don't lean into the mud! Your arms might get trapped."

Fastening one end of the come-along to a fence post, he ran the ratchet cable out as far as he could. When it was stretched to its length, he attached the rope and tossed the looped end of it toward Cilla.

"Put the loop around the calf. Not its neck, as that will choke it. Slip one end behind its rump, under the tail and as far down his hips as you can. That's it. Now put the slipknot in front of its chest." Watching as she clumsily followed his directives, Thomas backed up until he was next to the ratchet. "If you can, help work his legs free as I tighten this and pull him out."

Please Gott, *let this work. If it doesn't, I'm afraid I'll lose both of them.* "All right. Here we go."

The come-along slowly clicked beside him as he worked the ratchet. The cable and rope tightened. The calf's eyes bulged. Its mouth gaped as it released a wretched bawl. Cilla's sob joined it as she reached into the muck to free it. Thomas caught his breath, fearful, even though he'd advised it, that her efforts would result in trapping her further. He worked the ratchet as fast as he dared. It was hard to tell what was calf and what was mud coming out of the muck. With a mighty bawl, the calf finally slithered free of the bog's clutch.

Thomas carefully winched it closer until he could pull it onto firmer ground. Slicking the mud from its legs, he quickly freed the calf from the rope and slid it in the direction of its frantic mother. He'd check it over later.

Now to get to his granddaughter.

Muddy rope in hand, he hurried back to the churned-up muck. "All right. This time you." He slung the rope to her. It landed on the deceptive surface a foot in front of her chest. Although Cilla reached for it, her movements were awkward. She couldn't judge the distance. She was shaking so hard she couldn't get her hand on the rope, much less get it around her.

He had to get out to her. He eyed the ground between them. *Nee, nee,* he couldn't try it. Two steps in and all options would be gone for them. Again, he frantically scanned the area. He needed something to spread his weight on. His gaze landed on the branch he'd tried earlier. Too narrow. Too likely to roll with him. A bigger branch hung from a nearby tree. He quickly dismissed it. Too big to break, and he didn't have a saw. Cilla's face was pale. Her chest was tilted precariously toward the muck. One hand was in it up to her wrist. If she tipped farther...

Thomas cast a longing look up the hill to the barn and his tools. He couldn't leave her to retrieve any. His gaze flicked to the cow reassuring her calf from the far side of the board fence. The top rail bowed as the Jersey pressed against it. Dashing to the fence, Thomas pushed against the rail. It creaked but didn't move. Solidly built to protect the livestock from the creek, he now needed it loose to use it on what he'd protected them from.

Moving to where the next rail was nailed to the post, he closed his eyes. "Please *Gott*, you made me a strong man. Help me be stronger yet." Backing up, he charged the fence and slammed his shoulders, broad and strong from years of blacksmithing, against the rail near the post. The nail shrieked as the board gave a bit. Backing up, Thomas smashed into it again. On the third blow, he plunged partway over the remaining fence when the top board gave. The other end of the rail came off in a single blow.

Thomas hustled the board to where Cilla

shivered in the mud. He shuffled it out as far as he dared. Bracing one end on firm ground near him, he worked the other to a high tuft of grass that stood above the green-tinged bog just in front of where Cilla was mired.

Retrieving the rope, he attached the end of it to his suspenders and eased himself onto his belly over the board. As he crawled forward, his knees skimmed the muck. He hissed in a breath when the board wobbled under him. Slowly, the distance between Cilla and him shrank. The suspenders dug into his shoulders as the rope tightened behind him. *Please let it have enough length to reach her.* He risked a glance at his granddaughter. Her eyes were on him, hope and fear battling in their depths. Locking his jaw, Thomas inched forward.

"I'll get you out. I will get you out."

Chin quivering, she nodded. Her gaze moved over his shoulder, and her expression brightened. "Look! Bambi's on his feet. He looks okay."

At the moment, Thomas didn't care about the calf. His concern was for the animal's valiant rescuer. "He's more than okay. You saved him. Foolishly, I might add. But very bravely. Now we have to get you out before you become a human icicle and I just store you in my ice house all summer to keep my produce cool."

Cilla's faint giggle became a hiccuping gulp. "You wouldn't do that."

"I might. I was that scared when I found you. And that irritated when you wouldn't let me get you out first." Thomas worked while he talked, cautiously reaching behind him to unfasten the rope without tipping the board. "But you're right. I won't. You'd probably thaw out halfway through the summer, and I'd have to find something else anyway. And you'd probably want the cat in there with you, warming you up even faster, as furry as that thing is."

"Flower does have long fur, doesn't she?" Her voice quavered. "I wish I could hold her right now."

Thomas looped the rope into position under her arms, the knot centered on her chest, appearing pathetically frail under the sodden material. It wasn't what he wanted, but it was all the length he had to work with. He wished he could give her his shirt as padding, but there was no way to remove it without risking his precarious perch on the board.

He forced a smile. "I'm not sure she'd want you to until you've scraped off some of the muck. She seems a finicky animal. Always cleaning herself. She cough up any hairballs yet?"

He was rewarded with a little giggle. "No."

"*Ach*, if she does, I'll get you your own shovel. You can start assisting with the barn chores."

"I'd like that." His heart ached as her teeth chattered on the whisper.

"I have to go back to work the ratchet. But I'll be right there. We'll do this together." He held her gaze. "I wish it wouldn't. But it's going to hurt."

"I understand."

She reached for his hand, tears welling in her eyes. He gave it a reassuring squeeze. The trust in her eyes overwhelmed him. Love for this child surged through him. Gott, *please let this work. Please help me get her out and do so without hurting her worse.* When he reluctantly loosened his grip, Cilla clutched at it. Her slender throat bobbed in a hard swallow. She bit her lip and finally let go to grasp the rope.

Easing back over the board, Thomas held his breath when it bowed and creaked under him. He slid a fraction farther. The board tipped. Fetid swamp smell wafted up as his elbow dipped into muck. His heart pounded as he fought the urge to curl his fingers under the board's far side, an action that could over-balance and flip it, and him, into the mud. Spread-eagling his legs, he finally regained his balance.

When his knees hit dry ground, Thomas quickly scrambled the rest of the way off. Hurrying to the come-along, he cautiously took up any slack. "Lean on the board. Pull it toward you. Work to get on top of it as soon as you can so it can help support you. Understand?"

Cilla dipped her chin in a shallow nod. Thomas inhaled a shuddering breath and moved the lever, the responding click ominously loud in his ear. Cilla's face contorted as the wire and rope stretched tight between them. With each click, he heard her whimper. It made him ill to put her through such pain, but he had no other options.

When she had her upper torso on the board, he stopped and wiped the sweat from his forehead. "Let's rest for a moment."

"It's all right, Grandpa." Tears were creating rivulets through her mud-streaked face. "I know you have to do it."

For the first time since Priscilla had died, Thomas fought his own tears. If he could've reversed places, he surely would have. "All right. Let's finish this. We'll get you up to that furry cat."

After what seemed an eternity, she was fully on the board. Thomas left the come-along and carefully brought in the rope until Cilla was close enough to pull into his arms. Freeing her from the muddy loop, he scooped her up and cleared the shortened fence to stride up the hill with his precious bundle. The journey never seemed so long.

Halfway up it, Cilla tapped his shoulder and pointed. He looked over to see the Jersey calf trotting along at his mother's side. Thomas took his first deep breath since he'd left the shop. If the calf, which'd presumably been in longer than Cilla, was all right, then hopefully she'd be as well. He'd heard stories that extensive pressure on the limbs could cause even more problems for the body when the pressure was released.

"How long were you trapped?"

From the cradle of his arms, Cilla furrowed her brow. "Not that long until you came. Just long enough for me to forget I was mad at you."

Thomas grunted. "I know you're stubborn like me. If your temper's like mine as well, you must've been there for some time then." Upon reaching the farmyard, he carried her shivering form straight to his shop.

He knew how quickly he could heat up his forge. When it was blazing to his satisfaction, he raced to the house for a blanket, a towel, clean clothes and a bucket of water to heat, along with a pitcher to drink. To his relief, nothing seemed broken or dislocated from the interlude. Even so, as she warmed up, the pain in her legs increased. At each whimper, Thomas flinched.

When she finally stopped shivering, he asked quietly. "Do you need to see a doctor?"

Cilla shook her head. "No. I'll be okay. If you'll bring me Flower." She looked at him with a dipped chin and a spark of what he'd grown used to seeing in her eyes. Thomas knew he was being manipulated. He didn't care.

"What if Flower doesn't want to come into the shop?"

"Oh, I think she will. And it would be so warm and comforting to have her purring on my lap."

His mouth tilted. "There's still time to stick you in the icehouse. You haven't thawed out completely yet."

"You wouldn't do that." Tipping her head, she studied him. "You also wouldn't have left me out in the creek."

"*Nee*. I wouldn't have. Next big rain, you might've washed down to the bridge. Then what would my neighbors think." He felt the weight of her attention on his back as he turned to tend the forge.

"Why didn't you ever visit me when I was little?"

Thomas went still. His throat was suddenly dry. His voice, when he could speak, was hoarse. "I didn't know about you." He poked at the fire. "I wish I had."

"Why didn't you visit my mom? You knew about her."

Inhaling sharply, he turned to face her. "I didn't know where she was. I should've tried harder to find out. I'll never not know where you're at." Uncomfortable with the emotions that churned in him, he lowered his brow in a fierce scowl. "As long as you tell me where you're going before you disappear."

Cilla reached up to lay a hand against his whiskered chin. "I promise."

It was solemn. And so was the vow Thomas made to himself. Whatever it took, he was going to find a way to keep her.

Chapter Nine

Emma's heart beat in cadence with Cricket's trotting hoofbeats as she drove the mare up the lane. After a visual sweep of the farmyard, her eyes flicked between the blacksmith shop and the barn for any indication of movement. Their doorways, open like that of her buggy on the pleasant spring day, remained empty. *What are you going to do if he comes out, Emma? It's not like you're turning around and driving back out the lane before you see how Cilla is doing.* No, she wasn't. So with a tight chest and a gaze that continually swiveled between the open doors, she drew the mare to a halt.

Quickly descending, she hustled to secure the mare before returning to the buggy. Withdrawing a casserole dish and a bag, she hurried to the house. *What are you going to do if he's inside? What are you going to do if he's not? It's a small community. You can't avoid him forever. In fact, you'll see him in church on Sunday. With the women sitting on one side and the older men sitting toward the front on the other, he'll be hard to miss. Then there's fellowship afterward. What are you going to do then? Duck into the kitchen? Hide in corners? Maybe it's better to face him now and get it over with.* Emma gnawed on her lip as her gaze swung to the lane and the all-too-vivid memory of the distressing walk home a few days ago. *I'll face him when I have to. And not before.*

Balancing the casserole and bag in one hand, she knocked softly on the screen door with the other. Upon hearing Cilla's cheery "Come in," Emma took a deep breath, opened the door and stepped inside.

"I hear you had quite an adventure the other day." Heading for the refrigerator, she opened it and slid the casserole onto one of the many empty shelves. When she'd come through the door, a glimpse of Cilla's smiling face, dwarfed by the big chair she sat in, did a great deal to relieve her concern upon hearing the community grapevine's account of the girl's frightening experience. The obvious absence of Thomas further slowed her heartbeat to something resembling steady.

"Your first lesson in cooking, when you feel like getting on your feet. The casserole goes into the oven for an hour at 350 degrees. Don't forget to use potholders when you pull it out." Emma headed down the hallway toward the bedrooms with the bag. "I'll be right back." She smiled over her shoulder.

She paused briefly outside one of the bedroom doors, the bag clutched to her chest. Turning the knob, she entered and closed the door behind her. On the occasions she'd cleaned the house, even though it was unused with the door resolutely shut, she'd always come in to dust what used to be Priscilla and Thomas's bedroom. Her friend had been an adept housekeeper, and Emma couldn't let the room look abandoned. Crossing to the oak dresser and opening a drawer, she carefully retrieved the apricot dress from the bag and placed it inside. With a final stroke of the material, she slid the drawer shut with a sigh. It couldn't undo what'd transpired, but returning the laundered dress to where it belonged removed a weight from her shoulders and her heart. Leaving the room, she quietly pulled the door shut behind her.

Cilla's head was craned in her direction when Emma returned to the living area. Interestingly, although there were other upholstered chairs available, the girl was sitting in the one Emma knew Thomas always used. To her surprise, a black-and-white kitten was nestled on Cilla's lap.

"I'm assuming this is Flower?" Emma raised an eyebrow. "In the years I've known him, your *grossdaddi* was never one to condone animals in the house."

Cilla's grin was sheepish. "I told him I'd be more comfortable and less lonely with the company."

"I suppose he figured the cat was better than trying to bring the calf inside."

"I did kind of mention Bambi first. To make sure he was doing okay."

Emma shook her head at the girl's audacity. "I'm sure his *mamm* will take *gut* care of him. And you? Are you doing all right?"

Careful not to disturb the dozing kitten, Cilla shifted slightly. "My hips are kind of sore. And my legs look a little puffier than they normally do. Grandpa was asking me all sorts of questions about how I was feeling. Said a bunch of times that maybe we should go to the doctor. But I think I'm okay."

Emma glanced at where the girl's legs, visible below the long hem of her dress, were propped on a cushioned ottoman.

"They've gone down from what they were

after Grandpa pulled me out. He says I need to learn to do laundry or sew to keep up with all the clothes I'm getting dirty." Cilla didn't seem offended by the suggestion.

Emma's lips twitched. "I imagine that's his way of saying he's glad you're safe."

"I'm kind of learning that. Seems like a backward way of doing things. So why doesn't he just say it?"

"*Gut* question. But that's the way your *gross-daddi* is."

Cilla stroked the sleeping kitten. "He's maybe better than I thought."

Emma had to swallow to get past her own hurt regarding Thomas. "I know he's trying."

"He's been nice to me for the most part." The girl's solemn blue eyes held Emma's reluctant gaze. "But he wasn't very nice to you."

Emma crossed her arms over her chest. "He still misses your *grossmammi*. He doesn't want to be disloyal to her." *I knew that. Neither do I. So why did his words hurt so much?*

"She's gone." The girl's voice was soft. Emma understood it wasn't so much a flat statement but a request to understand.

Rubbing a hand over her elbow, Emma looked about the room. The only thing that had changed in the past four years was the presence of the girl in the chair. "Not in his heart. Your *mamm* may no longer be here, but is it easy to envision another in her place?"

"No." This answer was quieter yet. Cilla's hands curled around the kitten as if to take comfort from the small bundle. Or maybe to protect it?

"It's the same for your *grossdaddi*." Which is why, although the cut hurt, Emma had needed it before she nurtured any more foolish hopes. Thomas would never change. His reaction had finally pushed her in a different direction.

Susannah had worked amazingly fast. When Henry Troyer stopped by the shop yesterday afternoon to ask if she'd join him for supper tonight, Emma had braced a hand on one of her shelves to keep from falling over in shock. The matchmaker's speed had been a *gut* thing, as Emma had entertained second, third and even fourth thoughts about her visit. Something Susannah probably anticipated.

Wanting to keep her mind off the upcoming event that she'd put into motion, Emma perched, careful to avoid disturbing Cilla's legs, on the edge of the ottoman. Speaking in the language Amish learn from birth, she commented, "I noticed the other day that you understood a little of our dialect?"

Dipping her chin, the girl lowered her eyes. *"Ja."*

"Your *mamm* teach you?"

"Ja. I think she was homesick for it."

"Why didn't you let someone know when you arrived that you knew the language?"

Cilla shrugged. "No one asked. There were already so many changes. And I didn't want to go to school. I'd changed schools a bunch of times before. It's not easy this late in the year when everyone already has their group of friends. I was afraid I wouldn't make any." She met Emma's sympathetic gaze. "Deciding not to have any friends is better than wanting them and them deciding they didn't want you. It was obvious when I showed up that Grandpa didn't want me. I figured everyone else would be the same."

Impulsively, Emma reached a hand toward the solemn girl. Cilla grasped it with both of hers, squeezing it for a moment as if it were a lifeline.

"Well, I don't race sticks, or wallow in the mud, with just anyone."

Moisture shimmered in the backs of the girl's eyes. "You're the best friend I've had in a long time."

With a hard swallow, Emma blinked back her own tears. Returning the squeeze, she gradually let go and returned her hand to her lap. Surreptitiously rubbing the sore joints of her fingers, she gave Cilla a tilted smile. "Regardless of what he thought when you arrived, I know your grandpa wants you now. I'm glad he has you, and you have him. And Flower. And your calf. Bambi is it? You've gathered quite a collection in the short time you've been here. Thomas might have to build a new barn to hold everything by the time you're done."

Cilla's expression brightened. "I'm hoping for a pony too."

Emma's smile widened. "I don't blame you. Give it a bit of time." She pushed up from the ottoman. "Which is something I don't have today. I need to get back to open the shop."

"Will you come over and join us for the supper you brought? To make sure I do it right?"

"I can't. I have a beau coming over this evening." Emma blushed at the admission, feeling fifteen instead of forty-five.

Cilla lowered her strawberry blond eyebrows. "A beau?"

The flush spread across Emma's cheeks and down her neck. She'd hurried over this morning out of concern for Cilla. But she'd welcomed the extra distraction. In fact, she'd made a long list of chores to keep her busy today so she didn't think about tonight. For the first time in decades, she had a man coming over to take her to dinner. Just the reminder caused her palms to sweat. "*Ja*. A…neighbor and I are going out to eat."

"You have a *date*?" It sounded like an accusation as the girl's brows lowered farther. "Was this set up by one of the match ladies? The ones that put people together?"

Emma's embarrassment spread to her ears, causing them to burn. She was discussing her romantic life, or lack thereof, with a ten-year-old. "*Ja*, the matchmaker suggested him."

"What makes this guy so special?"

The fact that he's not your grandfather. Emma restrained herself from blurting out the response, one that would only prompt more questions. "He's a nice, respectable man. He works hard."

From Cilla's expression, those weren't impressive characteristics. "Why'd she choose him for you?"

"His wife died a few years ago. He farms." He was also the only one of the few single men her age in the district to express interest, but the young girl didn't need that information.

"He coming to pick you up?"

This was as difficult as Emma had anticipated it would be to tell Elizabeth of her plans. Which is why she hadn't told her sister yet. "He'll be over after he finishes chores."

"Are you going to marry him?"

"Goodness! Not after one outing." Maybe not at all. The prospect was startling. Although that *was* the reason she'd gone to see Susannah. But thinking of anyone other than her guilty dreams of Thomas in that role still seemed...odd.

"Huh." The kitten was awakening, blinking open its eyes, stretching out its front legs. Cilla ran a finger over the dainty white paws.

It seemed like a good time to make a quick exit before the girl thought up more embarrassing questions. Emma headed for the door with a wave. "I'm so glad to see you recovering well. Don't forget, 350 degrees for an hour."

Cilla smiled. "I won't forget anything."

Keeping a wary eye on the smithy, Emma darted to her buggy. With nerves already bubbling like a full pot over a fire with her upcoming date and the grilling by Cilla, it only needed an encounter with Thomas to boil over. Thankfully the shop door remained empty as she scrambled into the buggy and turned the horse down the lane.

She needed to turn her mind from the one who'd never come courting to the one who was. Henry was coming over this evening. She had no idea what she was going to say to him after he arrived beyond *Guten Dagg*, which wouldn't make for a very long, or stimulating, conversation.

Before Henry arrived, she needed to tell her sister about her plans. Other than a hamburger joint, the Dew Drop, where Elizabeth ran the kitchen, was the only place to eat in town. Elizabeth was working this evening. By the time Emma sat down and received a menu, word would have swept through the restaurant, and probably the district, that Emma Beiler was eating out with a man.

The ensuing conversation with her blunt sister would be better in their own kitchen rather than in the one at the Dew Drop, or worse yet, in the restaurant's dining area. So when Emma reached home, she tended the mare with a jumpy stomach. With dragging feet and sweaty palms, she climbed the porch steps.

Elizabeth looked over from where she was kneading dough when Emma entered the kitchen. "You've been out early the past few mornings."

Rubbing the back of her neck, Emma looked longingly at her shop door and the peace and security of disappearing through it. "*Ja.* This morning I went over to see how Cilla, Thomas's granddaughter, was doing after her episode in the creek yesterday."

Elizabeth pressed the heels of her hands into

the dough. "I'd heard about that at the restaurant last night. The grapevine is wondering how long she'll stay at Thomas's. Word is that she likes to run off."

After washing her hands, Emma got out the bread pans and began greasing and flouring them. "They might be getting along better than folks think."

With a noncommittal grunt, Elizabeth shaped the loaves.

Sliding a pan over, Emma asked with studied nonchalance, "What's the special tonight at the Dew Drop?"

Slipping a loaf-shaped section of dough into the pan, Elizabeth eyed her with a raised brow. "Why?"

Emma gave the pan she was preparing all her attention. "I might be in later tonight. I happened to see—" she winced at the simplification, but it sounded better than admitting that she'd sought the matchmaker out "—Susannah Weaver the other day. I asked her if she knew of...anyone." Elizabeth would know what she meant without having to say it. "Henry Troyer is coming by to take me to supper tonight," she finished in a rush.

She slid the prepared pan over. When nothing went into it for several moments, Emma peeked in Elizabeth's direction. Arms crossed, her flour-covered fingers tapping against the sleeves of her dress, her sister studied her. Flushing, Emma carried dirty dishes to the sink. She was a grown woman. That's why she'd done this. She didn't need her sister's permission to go out with a man. Elizabeth had always acted like she was years older rather than just a few minutes. Even as her frustration flared, Emma realized, more than seeking her sister's approval, she was apologizing for wanting to change the status quo they'd shared for decades.

"If you're going to walk out with someone, why not Thomas? You've been in love with him all these years."

Emma dropped the measuring cups from her hand. They clattered onto the linoleum floor, shooting flour and other baking residue in all directions.

"Did you think I wouldn't notice?"

Picking up the cups, Emma put them in the sink and ran water over a dishcloth, one she wanted to press to her heated cheeks. "Do you think Priscilla did?"

Elizabeth treated Emma's quiet query with the consideration it deserved. "I don't know. Priscilla was pretty observant. But even if she did, she wouldn't have felt threatened by it."

"Denki." Just what she needed; hearing that

she wasn't attractive enough to draw a man's attention was another blow to her confidence. Squatting, Emma wiped up the mess on the floor.

Her tone must've been evident. "I didn't mean it like that. I meant that she knew you'd never do anything to disrupt her relationship with Thomas. But Priscilla has been gone for years. So if you want to be courted, why not Thomas?"

Rinsing out the dishcloth, Emma set it aside to be laundered. "He'll never care for anyone but Priscilla. Anyone else would be a poor substitute in his mind. And, maybe I'm being *hochmut*—" she crossed her arms as well "—but I... I want more than that." Was it too proud to want to be seen and valued for yourself? To be someone's first choice? Maybe she'd eavesdropped on too many *Englisch* conversations in her shop. Read a few too many novels from the discount store. In her culture, *Gott* and the community always came first.

"I don't think it's wrong. Marriage is for life. I'd like to think you and I have attained some sort of satisfaction in our lives over the years. At least I hope so. As singles, we have freedoms that married Amish women don't have. I also hope it's not wrong to admit I'd feel left behind and miss you if you moved out."

Emma winced. "It's our first outing. Henry and I might not suit. I haven't seemed to with anyone before." She forced a wry laugh. "I'm a long way from moving out."

"We've made a *gut* team, haven't we?"

"*Ja*, and even if something works out for me, it doesn't mean we still won't be. It's a small community. I'd never be very far away."

"It still wouldn't be the same."

Elizabeth's face twitched. Emma recalled with chagrin that Elizabeth had had a beau once, one that'd seemed like he was headed for marriage. Although she'd felt selfish about it at the time, Emma had been glad that, for whatever reason, the relationship hadn't worked out and the man had moved to Ohio. Otherwise, she would've been alone in taking care of her *daed* the months he'd been ill before he'd passed. And then, just…alone.

Theirs wasn't the life either of them had dreamed of, but she and Elizabeth had gotten along all right. Although they were twins, they'd never been as close as they had in the last few years after Priscilla was gone. Elizabeth was right. They had a level of independence many women in their culture didn't have. Why did she want to change that now? Her sister seemed content, even happy, ruling her domain, running the kitchen in the Dew Drop.

But Emma was no longer content. No longer satisfied with things remaining the same. *Am I embarrassed by my unmarried state in a community where families are so valued?* Yes, Thomas had made her feel like she was something unwanted throwing herself at him. Why wasn't she satisfied with what had always been? Or was it Cilla? In getting acquainted with the little girl, had she discovered what she'd missed in not having a family?

She remembered Susannah Weaver resting a hand on her stomach with a mixed expression of wonder and trepidation. If it wasn't too late for Susannah, was there still a chance for her if she were to marry soon? Henry might not be courting to have more children, but that didn't mean she might not be able to give him a child. At least Henry was the one seeking *her* out, not accusing her of chasing *him*. It was a balm to the pride she knew she shouldn't have.

Turning back to the counter, she nudged a pan toward where more shaped loaves rested on the counter. "As I said, we might not suit. In fact, it's doubtful we will. After all these years of living without a man, it might be a little too much work to figure out how to live with one." She smiled at her sister. "Still, it's a night out with a *gut* meal."

"I don't know. Maybe if the meal's not so *gut*, one date is all it will be."

"You think too much of your cooking to do that."

Elizabeth gave a curt nod as she settled a loaf into a pan. "*Ach*, you're right. If he keeps coming around, I might have to come up with something to discourage him though."

Thomas gathered the twine in his hand after shaking the last of the straw bales into the horse stalls. He looked over in surprise to find Cilla in the open barn doorway. His brows immediately furrowed. "Are you all right?"

"*Ja.*" A jolt always shot through him when she used their dialect. "I was just bringing Flower back to the barn. Thanks for letting me keep her in the house today."

A cat in the house was a small price to pay for his guilt over Cilla's ordeal with the calf. He scrutinized the girl silhouetted in the doorway. Although she didn't look happy, he could tell, with his trained eye in checking livestock, that the swelling had diminished throughout the day to be almost nonexistent.

"I was wondering…since she came over to check this morning to see how I was doing, could we go over to Emma's house now that you're finished with chores to show her that

I'm even better? I don't want her to worry about me."

Stifling his immediate response to deny the request, Thomas rocked back on his heels. He needed to apologize. It was best to get it out of the way. Waiting would only make it an even more difficult task. He'd seen Emma arrive today. To his dismay, he'd ducked deeper into his shop to unnecessarily sort tools at his back bench. He'd never thought of himself as a coward. It was a label he didn't care for.

But when he'd finally worked up his resolve, Emma had dashed out of the house like a fast-ball from a strong-armed pitcher. By the time he'd reached the door, the orange slow-moving vehicle triangle on the back of her buggy was retreating down the driveway.

She didn't know he'd lashed out at her over guilt. So he'd spent part of his day making her a gift, a nutcracker comprised of a solid metal hinged device attached to a nice walnut base. All Emma had to do was press down on the handle to crack a nut without applying finger pressure. Hopefully the gift would help smooth the way for his apology. He considered his granddaughter's beseeching expression. *Ja*, might as well get it over with.

The casserole he'd seen Emma bring over would be safe in the refrigerator. Maybe, after she'd forgiven him, they'd get an invitation to supper tonight and spend the evening shelling walnuts again. He'd like to watch her use the tool he'd made for her. The thought warmed him more than the sunny day in the smithy had.

"*Ja.* Sounds like a *gut* idea. It might even be a *gut* time for your first driving lesson."

His mind on his upcoming apology, Thomas listened with half an ear to his granddaughter's chattering on the way over. As Banner trotted up the lane, Thomas's eyebrows rose at the sight of a horse and buggy hitched to the post. He glanced at the descending sun. It was well after hours for the shop. She shouldn't have any customers now. Of course, she could have visitors. Probably one of the other women from the community coming over to visit the Beiler twins. Thomas rubbed the back of his neck. Why would he feel so disappointed just because Emma wouldn't be alone? Maybe it was for the better. There would be a buffer beyond Cilla to help relieve the tension when they saw each other for the first time after he'd been such a bullheaded fool.

Cilla scrambled down from the buggy as soon as he drew Banner to a stop. Thomas descended at a much slower rate. As Cilla had already entered the house by the time he reached the door, Thomas, an apologetic smile on his face, pushed it open as well. His smile lowered at the sight of Henry Troyer, dressed in his almost Sunday best, seated at the kitchen table.

Chapter Ten

Thomas stiffened at the sight. He'd always liked Henry, whom he'd known all his life. He just didn't like seeing him in Emma's kitchen, sitting at Emma's table.

Why *was* Henry sitting so comfortably in Emma's kitchen? It surely wouldn't be a church matter? Thomas couldn't imagine, even as upset as she might be with him, that Emma would ever do anything to necessitate a disciplinary visit from the new minister.

He exhaled a breath he wasn't aware he was holding. Hmm. It was Elizabeth's kitchen as well. Maybe Henry had decided he needed a wife to support him in his new role? Maybe he was courting Emma's sister? Rounder than Emma, with a sharper attitude, Elizabeth was an interesting woman. Certainly every man enjoyed a woman who could cook well. And she had other qualities that would make her a *gut* minister's wife.

She just wasn't as attractive as Emma. To him anyway. Thomas rubbed a hand over his mouth. Of course, who was he to judge? No woman had been attractive to him for the past few years—until several days ago.

Ja, it made sense that Henry would be thinking of courting. He'd lost his wife recently. It'd been…*ach*, maybe not that recently. Amish men didn't tend to remain single for long. *Gut* for Henry. Elizabeth too.

As long as it was Elizabeth the man was courting.

Stepping through the door, Thomas pushed it closed behind him with a click. Looking to him from where he'd been watching Cilla greet Emma's cat with a scratch on the head, Henry nodded.

"*Guder Owed*, Thomas. *Wie bischt?*" He tipped his head toward Cilla with a smile, an acknowledgment the girl returned with a narrowed stare. "I'd heard your household had expanded. And about your recent adventure in the creek. I trust everyone is recovering well?"

"*Ja*. We've been rolling along together all right. She definitely has potential as a farmer." Even knowing it was wrong to be *hochmut,* Thomas's chest puffed out at his granddaughter's courage. "She saved our Jersey calf. I wouldn't have been able to do it."

"Did she now?" A farmer himself, Henry nodded in approval. Approval Cilla apparently didn't appreciate, as she scowled at the man.

Thomas frowned. He hadn't taken the girl much into the community yet. Although she'd been…animated with him, he'd never figured her for being rude. He lowered his brows at her in admonition. To his surprise, and relief, she cleared her expression and refocused her attention on the cat.

Henry apparently caught the exchange. "There's no doubt she's your *kinskind*. You both gave me the same look. Am I traveling somewhere where I shouldn't? I figured as Susannah stopped by, there wasn't any existing understanding. If there is, I have to say I'm disappointed—" he gave a rueful smile "—but I can certainly understand and wish you all the best."

Although he'd always been neighbors with Elizabeth, she'd not been a part of his life like Emma, his wife's lifelong friend, had. Or a major part of his mind lately, like her sister. "*Nee*. No understanding."

Smiling in obvious relief, Henry nodded his head. "*Gut*. Because I'm hoping to maybe have one soon. I can't believe we've overlooked Emma Beiler all these years. I was more than pleased when Susannah mentioned she might be interested in walking out."

Emma was interested in walking out? Thomas felt his jaw drop like his beard was suddenly weighted with a fifty-pound bag of feed. She'd never given any indication she was interested in walking out. Even though he'd accused her of pursuing him, he knew that'd been his guilt talking and not her actual actions. She'd *always* been single. And all of a sudden, she's walking out?

If she was interested enough in courting to get a matchmaker involved, why hadn't someone said something to him now that he was planning to remarry?

Thomas's pulse accelerated. How had he gone so fast from thinking of courting to planning to remarry? His jaw closed and tightened as he heard a door open down the hallway that branched off from the kitchen. Well, he hadn't gone as fast as Emma in her apparent race to the altar. One day she was there, as she always had been—friendly, supportive, hard-working, amusing…attractive. The next day, she's walking out with one of his neighbors—a neighbor who was already seeking an understanding. Had he just assumed she'd always be there, just because she always had been? Because *if* he was planning to remarry—Thomas's heart began to pound in earnest—*if* he was planning to remarry now that Priscilla was gone, he couldn't think of anyone other than Emma he'd want to consider as his wife.

But if that was his plan, he needed to get a move on, because Henry obviously wasn't at Emma's place to buy a hat. The evening certainly looked much different than what Thomas had anticipated on the way over, as did the future. In fact, he didn't like the way the future looked to be shaping up at all. Crossing to one of the empty chairs at the table, Thomas stiffly sat down. Tension hummed through him, his knee bouncing like an empty cart on a bumpy road.

Henry had asked if he and Emma had an understanding. Inhaling deeply, Thomas put a hand on his knee to stop its jittering before intentionally sprawling his legs to take up more room in the kitchen, one he'd been quite comfortable in a few evenings ago. He eyed the other man, who was eyeing him. He and Emma, an understanding? *Nee*.

Not *yet*.

At the sound of footsteps, he glanced down the hallway. Emma came into view. When she saw the gathering in her kitchen, she stopped like she'd run into a wall. Her face went from attractively flushed to reddening like a glowing ember in his forge. Her hand clamped over her mouth. Her eyes widened and swiveled between him and Henry at the table. For a moment, Thomas wondered if she was going to dash back down the hallway. She probably would've if Cilla hadn't drawn her attention.

"Grandpa and I wanted to show you that I was better."

Emma's voice was whisper thin. "I… I'm glad to hear it."

"I guess we can't stay for supper again because you're going out."

Thomas's eyes narrowed as he considered his granddaughter. The girl looked entirely too ingenious. But her words seemed to have broken Emma free of her stupefied state. "*Ja, ja*, I am. So *gut* to see you, Henry. Looks like you're ready to go. Me too. Right now, in fact." She walked right past Thomas to the front door.

Henry pushed up from his chair, a broad smile on his face as his gaze encompassed Emma, almost as if he couldn't believe his good fortune. Thomas rose more slowly. Although her gaze flickered once in his direction, Emma hadn't looked at him since that first aghast glance.

Thomas didn't mind doing all the looking. It wasn't hard to do. Neat and trim in her green dress, she looked very nice. Very unlike the mud-slathered woman he'd assisted the other night. Surprisingly, that woman was equally appealing to him. At least she'd been more accessible than this one, who didn't seem to want to acknowledge his presence. It was understandable. He owed her an apology—one that would have to wait. Wait for a time when another man wasn't escorting her out the door. And once he had that settled between them…

Thomas, along with Cilla, followed the pair out. He didn't remember the nutcracker he'd made until he saw it on the buggy seat as he climbed in. For the first time since he'd entered the kitchen, a hint of a genuine smile crossed his face. He'd soon find a time to deliver it— alone—to Emma, along with his apology. As Cilla scrambled into her seat, Thomas glanced across the yard to see Henry assisting Emma into the buggy. He scowled. Maybe along with his own dinner invitation.

"Can we go into town to the restaurant too?"

"Nee." Cilla's face fell at his abrupt response. Thomas scratched his chin. Although he knew there was a casserole in the fridge, he didn't feel like eating it when the hands that made it might be holding another man's hands tonight. His own hands tightened on the lines. No point in taking his mood out on his granddaughter though—he'd learned that much in the past couple of days.

He glanced over at her pensive face, then looked at her legs, dangling from the buggy seat. It was only yesterday that he'd been afraid he might lose her. His stomach twisted at the memory. He sighed. "*Nee*, but I suppose Banner could handle a trip into town tonight, and we might get a hamburger and shake at the fast food restaurant."

"Really!" Cilla bounced on the seat. "I've never done a drive-through with a horse and buggy!"

"Well…" Thomas hadn't planned to include the drive-through window in his spontaneous offer. At the end of the lane, he turned the buggy toward town. A flash in his side mirror revealed the couple behind them turned toward town as well. To go out to dinner. Maybe to begin an *understanding*.

"I haven't either. Why not?" He urged Banner into a brisk trot.

Emma doubted that her heart rate would ever return to normal. When she'd finally quit dilly-dallying and gathered her courage to join her date for the evening to discover not one, but two men in the kitchen—one of them the reason for the other—her heart had stopped. When it'd started up again, it'd jumped, skipped and raced. Now it just pounded as she watched Thomas's buggy turn not in the direction of his farmstead but toward town. The only places open this time of night in Miller's Creek were the restaurants. Surely he and Cilla weren't going to the Dew Drop as well?

She glanced over at her companion. As opposed to her bubbling nerves, Henry was calm and pleasant. He'd arrived before she was ready. At his knock on the door, in her unprepared panic, she'd hollered down the hall for him to come in with all the finesse of a farmer calling the cows home. Then when she'd stepped out to see the both of them sitting at her table… All she could think of was walking out through the shop door and not stopping until she was a day's buggy ride away.

And now it seemed they'd end up at the same spot anyway. Closing her eyes, Emma pressed a hand against her stomach. If it didn't stop jumping, she wouldn't be able to eat a bite tonight. Nerves taut, she'd entered her kitchen bracing herself for her first date in years, decades. When she'd seen Thomas sitting at the table, joy had surged through her as, for a heartbeat, it seemed a culmination of secret dreams coming true. But in the next heartbeat, the humiliation of his rejection came flooding back.

"Hungry?"

Her eyes shot open. *"Ja."* No. What was the

matter with her? She'd visited easily enough with Henry dozens of times on church Sundays and other community gatherings. Now she struggled with single word answers. And questions. "You?"

"*Ja*. Is your *schweschdere* cooking tonight?"

"*Ja*." Her response didn't share his enthusiasm.

Henry patted his own stomach. "Then everything will be *gut*."

Emma smiled weakly as she watched the buggy ahead pull farther away. Her breath hissed out in relief when it turned down a different road instead of continuing on to the street containing the Dew Drop. *Nee*. Everything wasn't good. At least not at the moment.

Courting wasn't like she'd imagined it to be.

Or maybe she wasn't like she'd imagined herself to be. The thought tugged at Emma as she descended the buggy. After all these years, she figured she'd enter a public place accompanying an obvious beau with a sense of excitement, enthusiasm and maybe a small, inappropriate amount of pride. She would finally have the sense of arriving in a community that sometimes unconsciously excluded from the family-based posture of Amish culture what they called "single sisters" or "leftover blessings." She felt none of those things.

Keeping her head down, she followed Henry to a booth. Scooting across the vinyl seat, she sat in a corner as out of sight of the rest of the restaurant as possible. Folding her hands in her lap, she took a deep breath as she returned a faint smile to her companion.

Her odd feelings weren't because of Henry. He was a handsome man, pleasant and respectable. With the exception of…well, with the exception of someone who'd made it plain he'd never be interested in her in that or most any other way, Henry was a wonderful choice in anyone's book. No wonder Susannah had contacted him first. He just wasn't *her* first choice.

The Amish waitress, Rebecca, set down menus and glasses of water with a smile. Her curious gaze advised Emma that Susannah didn't share her matchmaking business discussions with her daughter. "I'll be back in a minute for your orders. Unless you need more time?"

"*Nee, nee*, we'll be ready," Emma hastened to assure her. The last thing she wanted at the moment was to extend this outing—one she'd brought about by her actions. Stealing another glance at Henry, she consciously lowered her tense shoulders. Henry was a *gut* man, one who didn't deserve her flopping about on her wants and wishes like a fish jerked from creek to bank. *Try to act like the mature woman you think you are, Emma.*

"Do you have any favorites?" Looking up from studying his menu, Henry smiled at her.

"Ja." But Thomas and his *kinskind* were somewhere else in town. Emma slapped down the rogue thought. *Thomas doesn't want you. He made that plain. Get over him.* "I think I'll try something new tonight."

Henry nodded his agreement. "I like an adventuresome spirit."

Emma smiled weakly. She had no idea what she was going to order—other than her stomach to calm down. When Rebecca returned to their table, Emma slid her finger randomly down the menu to make a selection. The waitress's brow was furrowed as she paused beside Emma.

"Elizabeth requested that you order the meat loaf special tonight. She's trying something new. She wants your feedback later. She said doing something new isn't always a *gut* idea, and that it's *gut* to get advice before doing it again. Just in case."

Emma got the message. She just wasn't sure she could handle whatever her sister was planning to serve up. But she figured the special would be more palatable than Elizabeth's input on her social life.

Chapter Eleven

"Why are we having church in a barn?"

Emma's lips twitched at Cilla's whisper, one loud enough to be heard by those nearby on the benches lined up in the cavernous building.

Her response was much quieter. "The district members alternate having services in their homes to emphasize it isn't a building, but the body of believers who are the true church. Some homes, like Susannah's, aren't big enough to hold the whole district so the service is held in that family's barn or shop."

"Why are only the women sitting in here? Where are the men?"

"They're coming in now." Too soon for Emma's peace of mind. When Cilla had latched on to her prior to the women entering for service, Emma had been glad of the distraction the girl provided. Anything to not think about the two men she'd be facing for the hours of the service; one whom she'd had a pleasant evening with despite her early misgivings, an evening that might lead to many more and a future together, and the other who had made it plain she wasn't what he wanted, and yet—even mortified as she was—she couldn't get her heart to obey her head that *he* wasn't what *she* wanted.

Henry and Thomas filed in with the other men. Out of the corner of her eye, she saw that, upon taking his seat, Thomas was scanning the women's side. When his gaze landed on Cilla—and her—it stayed. Dropping her attention to her lap, Emma picked at a thread in the fabric of her apron.

It remained there until Cilla piped up again. "What's that man doing?"

Emma looked up as the solo notes of the first song rang out in slow procession. She opened the hymnal beside her. "He's the *vorsinger*. He leads the singing."

Cilla frowned at the book. "Where are the notes? Don't you have musical notes in your songbooks?"

"Not in the *Ausbund*."

"Then how do you know what to sing?"

"The tunes have been passed down for generations. We've been singing these songs for centuries."

"Is that why you sing them so slowly?"

Emma blinked as she struggled for an answer. Finally, smiling, she just shook her head.

Cilla squirmed throughout the church service, unlike the children who'd grown up there, accustomed to three hours on the hard backless benches every other Sunday morning. At times, Emma wanted to squirm herself at the girl's loud whispers. Other times she had to stifle an inappropriate laugh at her observations. But like a pebble in her shoe, she was aware of Thomas's constant attention. As soon as she realized her gaze had again landed on his unsmiling face, she'd fix her attention on something else. On one such occasion, she glanced at Cilla, who'd thankfully been quiet for all of ten minutes. It was a mistake, as the girl was looking straight at her, before glancing over at Thomas.

"Do you like my grandpa?" Her young voice seemed to resonate up to the barn's rafters.

Emma flushed so hot she was surprised she didn't melt into the wooden church bench. To her chagrin, not only Cilla's attention, but that of several of the surrounding women, was on her. She toed a piece of straw on the barn's otherwise immaculate concrete floor.

Sweat beading on her forehead, she murmured, "Thomas is my neighbor. *Gott* says we are to love our neighbors as ourselves." Emma inhaled deeply after the pious comment, relieved to have come up with a suitable answer, one that would hopefully end the conversation. Cilla narrowed her eyes and pursed her lips but nodded as if satisfied.

"Are all the Amish here?"

Shoulders relaxing fractionally at the abrupt subject change, Emma responded in a low voice, "Everyone in our *gmay*." When Cilla's brow puckered at the word, she clarified. "In our church district."

"Which one is the match lady?"

Emma snuck a glance to see what their seatmates thought of the conversation. Ruth and Gail Schrock were among those outright smiling, or trying to cover the fact that they were. Others were not so entertained. Reluctantly, Emma nodded toward Susannah, who was seated farther down the row. Cilla craned her neck to see the woman, shifting enough that she drew Susannah's attention.

Ruby Weaver was one of the unsmiling ones; no surprise, as smiles from the woman were like hen's teeth. Emma wondered if that would change if the bishop's wife knew about Susannah's news. With Jethro as their only child, they'd been against him marrying a woman ten years his senior. Emma glanced over at the men's benches to discover the man's gaze resting on his wife, a gentle smile on his face.

She bit the inside of her cheek. The sight made her melancholy. Jethro had found happiness in a mate. Would she ever find hers? As she was considerably older than him, the possibility seemed slim. Still... She slid her gaze down the opposing row to find Henry's attention on her, and when their eyes connected, he smiled. The corner of Emma's lips tilted up in response. Her heart beat a little faster. Was that happiness? Or panic? Was marriage in and of itself what she was seeking at this point in her life? Or was she seeking one with the happiness like Jethro had found in his own?

A service had never seemed so long.

Emma disappeared to the kitchen as soon as it was over. Having made the transition from service to meal every other Sunday for years, the women of the district seamlessly organized the changeover. Church benches were quickly rearranged into tables. In short order, the adult males were being served first. Emma jumped into any task that would keep her in the kitchen—and away from the tables and the men surrounding them.

She was portioning out desserts when Cilla tugged on the sleeve of her dress.

"They need more bread-and-butter pickles.

I looked in the basement like they said, but there're a lot of different kinds of pickles down there, and I don't know which is which. And I don't want to get it wrong the first time I'm helping."

Emma gave the girl an encouraging smile. Cilla had been very helpful indeed. Having followed the women into the kitchen, she'd immediately executed any task they'd asked. The girl had been carrying desserts out to the diners last Emma knew, but she wasn't surprised Cilla had been sent on another errand in the busy process of quickly feeding well over a hundred people.

"I'll run down and get some. How many jars?"

"Thanks. Maybe two? You have time to finish cutting that cake though." With an enigmatic grin, Cilla picked up two more plates, including one containing an edge piece Emma had set aside. The cake in that corner had been overdone, so Emma had trimmed out that piece, planning on leaving it in the kitchen.

"Wait—"

But the girl was already out the door. Emma shook her head and continued cutting and plating the pumpkin pie cake she was working on. It didn't matter. The desserts were set on a table to be chosen by the diners and that one wouldn't be. It would find its way back to the kitchen at the end of the day.

Thomas had been keeping his eye on Cilla as she scurried back and forth. Even way over on his side of the seating and above the minister's preaching, he thought he'd heard her voice during the service. Thankfully, most of the congregation was tolerant, knowing the situation and that this was her first Amish church Sunday.

He was also glad she'd been sitting by Emma. That'd given him the opportunity to gaze at his granddaughter—understandable—and see the woman beside her at the same time. Throughout the service, he'd discovered he wasn't the only one looking. He'd hidden a scowl behind his hand. The evening with Henry must've gone well, at least from Henry's perspective. So from Thomas's perspective, it made sense to stay close to Henry, to ensure today didn't go well enough that the new couple was on their way to an *understanding*.

Emma was a harder read. One time during the service, she'd turned bright red at something Cilla had said. He hadn't seen her since the service ended, but then, as he was keeping close to Henry, neither had her date from last night.

Were they planning to meet later? They might be beyond attending Sunday night singings, but Henry could still stop by Emma's place on his way home. Thomas's stomach did something funny at the thought of them being together again.

He looked up in surprise when Cilla appeared on the porch where he and Henry had been visiting about the prospects for a good hay year. But probably not as surprised as Henry looked when Cilla handed him the sorriest looking piece of cake Thomas had ever seen and stated, "Emma said to give that to you."

Turning abruptly to him, she continued. "Susannah asked me to get a jar of pickled beets from the basement, but they're on a shelf that's too high for me to reach. Could you go down and get it for me?"

Thomas raised an eyebrow at the odd request and the intensity on her young face. "*Ja.* I suppose I could."

"Could you do it now? I don't want the ladies to think I'm loafing."

As he wanted her accepted in the community, one which valued hard work and cooperation, he repeated, "*Ja.* I suppose I could." He gave a nod to Henry, who was dubiously considering the cake. Descending the porch steps, Thomas circled the house to the mud-room entrance, which from previous visits he knew led down to the basement where the canning was stored.

In the sunny early afternoon, the high windows of the basement allowed enough light that Thomas figured he could find the pickled beets without bringing down a lantern. Reaching the bottom of the wooden steps, he sighed in relief to find one of the women at the far end of the room. Surely, she'd have a better idea than him of the layout of the laden shelves.

The woman turned. Squeaking at the sight of him, she took a step back until she was blocked by the concrete wall. Thomas's mouth grew as dry as the slight layer of dust on a few of the jars that lined the shelves. He and Emma stared at each other across the width of the basement. After a few moments of silence, a cricket started chirping, apparently figuring the place had emptied out. Regrettably, the only thing empty was Thomas's mind.

He'd been planning to apologize. He needed to apologize. He also needed to practice these things, as he wasn't very *gut* with words and feelings and such. With the crowd at church today, he hadn't figured to get Emma alone. A bead of sweat trickled down his back under the jacket of his *mutza* suit. More than a bead coated his palms. What was he going to say? Nothing came to mind, at least nothing that he could share. When the last thing he'd told her was that she couldn't take Priscilla's place, he probably shouldn't blurt out that he'd suddenly decided that she could, and was hoping that she would. But he couldn't forgo this opportunity. Not when he'd been in the wrong and Henry had the inside path to developing an *understanding*.

The cricket must've felt the rising tension in the basement, as he stopped chirping. In the silence, Emma snatched two jars from a shelf and, making a wide circle around him, headed for the stairs. In another moment, she'd be up and out the door. If he didn't hurry, he'd miss his chance and only make things more difficult in the future.

"Why are you suddenly going out after all this time?" In his tension, the words sounded like an accusation, and they weren't the ones he'd wanted to say.

Halting abruptly, Emma stared at him, her mouth opening for a moment before compressing as flat as the top of his anvil. "Just because you don't want me, doesn't mean others don't."

"I mean, why are you doing it now? Just..." *Just when I realized...?* What had he realized? That he was finally ready to join the world again? That maybe he'd had enough of being alone? That being with someone else wouldn't really be a betrayal of Priscilla? That the someone else he wanted to be with was Emma, and no one else? And that if he didn't get in gear, he'd lose her?

He couldn't say that. But he couldn't not say anything either, so he waded in again. "I didn't mean what I said the other night. I mean, I meant it. You can't charm me." He intended to say something that a woman would want to hear; that surprisingly, she'd already charmed him without trying. But that's not what came out.

She shook her head. "Oh, Thomas, I doubt that you're capable of being charmed. No point in me wasting my efforts."

This wasn't going well. This was why he didn't try to talk about his feelings. Priscilla had always understood. Thomas's gaze fixed on Emma's affronted face a moment before it darted about the dim basement looking for inspiration. It landed on a shelf lined with quart jars of red-tinted contents. At least he could finish his errand sufficiently. Hastening over, he grabbed a jar of beets. Once his sweaty palm wrapped around the smooth glass, he turned back to find Emma had reached the basement steps. He had to stop her before she climbed them.

"I… I…um… You're not going to take Priscilla's place." Emma was making her own place in his heart, taking up considerable residence there. She'd already taken up a good share of space in his mind, although his pulse pounded and his stomach felt like it wanted to drop to the floor at the prospect of telling her.

Emma turned at his words. Her chest rose and fell with agitated breathing. Her voice was as tight as her white-knuckled stranglehold on the pickle jars. "I won't stop Cilla from coming over to my house, but *you* won't be bothered by me in the future."

Ach! This wasn't what he wanted at all. He should've just kept his mouth shut. Thomas flung up his hands in frustration. Momentarily forgetting the jar of beets, it slipped from his grasp and flew across the distance between them to land with a crash on the concrete floor in front of Emma. Chunks of beets and glass exploded at her feet. Beet juice splattered over Emma's apron and skirt like angry teardrops. The smell of vinegar permeated the room.

Thomas immediately started toward her. "Are you hurt?"

He paused in his rush when Emma held her jars of pickles in front of her like a shield. "*Ja.* But not like you mean." Setting the jars down, she shook out her apron and skirt and tapped the toes of her shoes to dislodge any debris. Retrieving the jars, she turned and stiffly mounted the stairs. The door shut behind her with a loud click, leaving Thomas in the basement with beets, a puddle of juice and a jar as shattered as he felt.

Chapter Twelve

The mailbox's metal door creaked as Emma opened it. Pulling out the newspaper, she closed the door with an uplifted elbow and unfolded the paper as she absently started up the lane. Her eyebrows rose at the stack of letters nestled inside. She flipped through them, expecting the bundle to be addressed to Current Resident. Drawing to a halt, she frowned in confusion when, with a variety of handwritings, they were all addressed to her. The unfamiliar return addresses offered no clues.

Tucking the newspaper under her arm, she slid a thumb under the flap of one envelope, slit it open and pulled out the single sheet inside. As she read down the page, her eyes widened. The newspaper tumbled unnoticed to the gravel as she fumbled to open another letter. Shaking her head in disbelief, she scanned the hand-printed lines.

By the time she'd made it to the house, she'd read them all. Sagging onto a kitchen chair, she retrieved the letters from their envelopes and studied them again before spreading them out on the kitchen table—making sure their envelopes containing return addresses were adjoined—and leaned back in her chair to stare at the collection.

Five men, ranging from nearby districts to an out of state address, wanted to court her. Five!

She'd never considered looking beyond her *gmay* for possibilities, but it made sense. Theirs was around twenty families, big enough to share the church services for the year and small enough that all attendants could fit inside someone's home or barn when they did. It was a small pond in which to fish for a mate. And Susannah had apparently determined to cast a wider net.

Emma giggled at the thought of drawing interested men in like fish. She giggled again for no reason at all. After all these years of being overlooked, to have five men—and that didn't include Henry—wanting to court her was overwhelming. She'd never felt this wanted. Picking up one of the letters, she fanned her face with it.

She wasn't surprised to read that four were

widowers. Amish men—with the exception of the one who'd splattered her best dress and apron with beet juice a few days ago—were generally quick to remarry. Even so, some were reluctant to blend families and preferred a never-married woman rather than a widow with children. Still, after all these years, she'd never figured to be that woman.

How was she going to respond? One was easy; she'd already decided to decline, just from the tone of the letter, but the others? Certainly she'd respond that she'd received their note. But to encourage them? Establish a correspondence?

She fanned the letter in front of her face faster. Wasn't that why she'd started on this path in the first place? To finally get her mind off of someone who'd made it more than plain that he wasn't interested? Setting the letter on the table with the others, Emma carefully smoothed the crinkled edge. She wished she wouldn't keep thinking about Thomas since their basement episode Sunday, but if wishes were horses on that topic, she'd rival Samuel Schrock, the local horse trader, for the number of equines that passed through his farm.

When she'd taken the pickles—the unnecessary ones she'd learned—upstairs, Emma had smiled over gritted teeth and finished her tasks before convincing Elizabeth to head home early and making her excuses to a very understanding Susannah. Having taken a close look at her face—and dress—Elizabeth was surprisingly and refreshingly quiet on the trip. Upon reaching home, Emma had attended to the stains. Thankfully, she was able to get them out of her clothes.

But getting the accompanying words out of her mind wasn't as easy. She'd let herself be so hurt. Until the emotion was replaced by anger. At Thomas, and herself. At Thomas, for being such a grouchy recluse the past few years that he couldn't see beyond the end of his beard, and at herself for having wasted so many decades thinking of, or trying not to think of, him. From now on, she would think of other things.

Like the surprising letters in front of her.

She flicked a finger through the envelopes, biting her lip as she contemplated the return addresses. She'd never thought about moving out of state, or even out of the district. Could she? Courting by letter wasn't unheard of. Maybe not in their *gmay*, but she'd heard of paths to remarriages that'd proceeded entirely through the mail. Was that something she'd allow herself to do?

Perhaps she should, *if* the man was right.

The only way to find out, it seemed, was to

respond to these unexpected letters. Gingerly putting them in order, Emma took them into her bedroom to secure in her dresser. Another thing she should do if she was going to proceed with this literary courting—make sure she picked up the mail before her sister did.

Thomas drew Banner to a halt and set the brake. Although his heart pounded, his shoulders rose in a relieved sigh to see no other buggies present. At least he'd be able to offer his apology to Emma in private. In her own shop, she'd be less likely to walk out the door, although it was still possible.

With a smaller sigh, he took off his straw hat and studied it with a frown. It'd been a *gut* hat. He could probably get the whole summer out of it. But it needed to serve a purpose today, which it couldn't do as is. With his index finger, he poked at a small hole in its crown and wiggled until his finger popped through. He added a second finger and wiggled some more. By the time he was satisfied, the tiny perforation the hat had when he'd driven up the lane was now a big hole.

His attention shifted to the bag on the seat beside him. Better try the apology first and then the gift. He'd probably waited too long as it was, but after his Sunday blunders, it'd taken him until now to work up his nerve to try again.

Maybe he should've brought her a new apron or dress to replace the ones he'd ruined? Thomas rolled his eyes; a dress was what'd gotten him into this situation in the first place. *Nee*, better stick to what he knew and hopefully she'd like it, as he was a failure at words. He could more easily fill up her toolshed with new or repaired tools than say an appropriate sentence, it seemed.

Ragged hat in hand, he climbed out of the buggy before he could lose his nerve and turn Banner back toward home.

It wasn't a good omen when, upon looking up at the door's cheery chime, Emma's smile quickly faded when she saw who was entering her shop. Her gaze flicked from him to the doorway. Her brow lowered when he closed it behind him.

"Cilla isn't with you?"

"*Nee.*"

"Is she all right?"

"I think so. She's over at the Zooks' playing with little Joanne."

"If she's not with you, then why are you here?"

Thomas lifted his hat with the finger poking through the hole. "You told me I needed a new hat a while back. I came to get one."

For a moment, she didn't reply. "You better keep it." She nodded to the hat he was turning by the brim in his hand. "I'll get you some tape to put over the hole."

Thomas blinked. Not sure he'd heard her correctly, he cocked his head. "What?"

"I don't think I can help you. I doubt I have a hat in the store big enough to fit the ego that seems to swell your head."

Thomas blinked some more. This wasn't the response his sweet Priscilla would've given him the times he'd needed to apologize to her. But it was a measure of how much his words had hurt Emma. The straw brim of the hat crinkled under a grip tightened by remorse. Would tape cover a fractured brim as well? By the time he apologized, he'd have the sorriest looking hat in the state of Wisconsin.

"*Ach*. I suppose I deserve that. And you *can* help me. You can forgive me for how foolish I was that night." He didn't have to explain which night. It was the one that'd wrecked a relationship that'd been balanced until he'd had thoughts that'd unbalanced it.

Folding her arms over her chest, she scowled at him.

"And again on Sunday. I am truly sorry."

She considered him through narrowed eyes.

"I'd have to dig around, but I might be able to find one that could work for you."

Recognizing it as an acceptance of an apology, or at least the beginning of one, the tightness in Thomas's chest eased. It'd been easier than he'd hoped. With something close to a bounce in his step, he followed her petite figure down an aisle. When the bell at the door jingled, she turned and stopped abruptly to glance in that direction. Unable to halt his momentum, Thomas caught her shoulders before he bumped into her. Their simultaneous inhalations overrode the quiet "Hello?" from the unseen customer. Emma took a rapid step back. Breaking their locked gazes, she grabbed a hat from a nearby shelf and thrust it into his hands.

"Try this one," she muttered before ducking around him.

Tucking his abused hat under his arm, Thomas set the new one on his head and wandered to the end of the aisle to see who'd arrived. Other than frustration at being interrupted when he wished they weren't, it really didn't matter. Unless the arrival was Henry Troyer.

It wasn't. A rare smile crossing his face, Thomas nodded to the newcomer. Jethro Weaver was years younger than him, but the bishop's only son was proof that wisdom and character didn't need age to be had in abundance. Jethro returned a rare smile of his own. Thomas's eyes narrowed slightly as he recognized that Jethro, also a widower, seemed much happier since he'd remarried.

"I'm looking for something a little b-bigger than what he's wearing." Jethro's smile widened as his gaze lifted to the top of Thomas's head.

Reaching up, Thomas found where the hat Emma had handed him was perched, much like a tiny jockey on a racehorse, over his hair. Jerking it off, he discovered Emma had handed him a child's hat. Intentional? He darted a look in her direction. Although her attention was on Jethro, a smile played around the corners of her mouth.

"I'm sure I can find something that will work for you. Some customers are just difficult to fit. May I see what you currently have?"

Removing his hat, Jethro used it to gesture in Thomas's direction. "He was here b-before m-me. Are you sure you d-don't want to t-take care of him first?"

Emma flicked Thomas a look as she took the hat. "*Ja.* I'm sure. He can wait. Or even leave if he wants."

Now Thomas scowled. Apparently, his apology wasn't anywhere close to being accepted.

Jethro's raised eyebrows met his bowl-cut

bangs. His gaze shifted between the two of them. Emma didn't notice. She did a quick scan of the interior of Jethro's hat before handing it back and motioning him to follow her. "How're you doing? I haven't seen you for a while."

Their conversation became indistinct as they headed to the opposite side of the store. Thomas dropped his gaze to the hat in his hand. She hadn't seen Jethro, but she'd apparently seen his wife? Had their meeting been one of chance, or had Emma sought out the matchmaker? Henry had confided to him that Susannah told him Emma would be receptive to callers. Had she *requested* them? The child's hat began to crease under the pressure of his fingers. Thomas quickly popped the folds back out and returned the hat to a shelf.

He headed for where Jethro was trying on hats. If ones in that aisle fit the bishop's son, surely they would fit him as well. Besides, he'd be able to hear more of their conversation. He doubted Emma would talk about matchmaking business with Susannah's husband, but how was he to know if he was on the opposite side of the room?

Ten minutes later, sporting a new hat, Jethro left. He eyed the two of them and shook his head as he went out the door. It shut behind him with a jingle that quickly died into silence.

Emma studiously ignored him as she fiddled with the receipt at her counter. Finally, Thomas set his roughed-up hat, along with a new one that had a similar fit, on the counter in front of her. "Do you have time for me now?"

"I don't know. I was under the impression that you didn't want my attention."

Ouch. Thomas winced at how he'd sabotaged decades of their neighborly relationship. Although he now wanted more—much more—he might be fortunate to resurrect even that. Shifting his feet, he lifted his hands in supplication. "I was a dunderhead. I said things I shouldn't have and didn't mean."

"Then why did you say them?"

Thomas closed his eyes on a deep inhalation. Could he admit to her that the feelings he'd been having for her unsettled him? Feelings that made him feel guilty regarding Priscilla? She'd been his special someone. His one and only. And now…now he couldn't get thoughts of Emma out of his head. When he was working, when he was trying to sleep, when his granddaughter said something funny and he knew Emma would enjoy it. That a slow, impish smile would bloom across her face? That *he* wanted to sometimes be the one to cause that smile and not just his granddaughter?

How could he tell her that when he was obviously uncomfortable with the feelings himself? What if it made her uncomfortable? What if it made her leap into a relationship with Henry because she was worried Thomas would be just what he'd accused her of? *Ach!* It was so much simpler to have had an understanding with Priscilla from before they were even teenagers. He was too old for this.

But he knew from his work that if you didn't bang on the metal, it'd never become what you wanted. Though you didn't get there right away. He had to repair their original relationship before he tried to coax Emma into something more, and to do that, she needed to know why he'd foolishly lashed out.

Hoping the right words would somehow reach the tip of his tongue when they hadn't even fully formed in his mind, Thomas inhaled a breath deep enough to fill the bellows back in his blacksmith shop. "It was because of what I was…feeling." He cringed like he was having a tooth pulled out by a pair of pliers. "Because I was…um…beginning to—"

They both jumped when the door to the house opened, and Elizabeth stepped into the shop.

Chapter Thirteen

Emma's heart was pounding. Thomas? Talking about feelings? What had he been about to say? And what would her *schweschdere* say? Holding her breath, her gaze swiveled between the two. From Thomas's face, she could tell whatever he'd been going to say had dried up like a garden in a drought at Elizabeth's arrival.

Regret surged through her. Which seemed to rekindle the tiny ember of hope that never seemed to go out. What if he finally saw her… *Oh, Emma, you are such a fool. Just be indifferent to him and be done with it.*

But frustratingly, she couldn't be. And now, Thomas wouldn't speak and Elizabeth likely would. At the moment, Emma wanted both of them out of her normally serene shop to give her some peace.

She turned to her sister. *"Ja?"* Her tone indicated it wasn't an invitation to linger.

Elizabeth's gaze rested on Thomas before shifting to her with a raised eyebrow. "I was wondering what your opinion was of the meat loaf special at the restaurant the other night."

Emma's eyes widened. "You're asking me *now*?"

"We never got around to discussing it." Elizabeth gave her a placid smile.

"Now is not *gut*."

"It's always *gut* to get advice when trying something new. Your efforts might not've worked out like you expected."

"I don't think anything is working out right now," Emma muttered, propping her hands on her hips as she considered her sister. "You want my opinion of the special. All right. The meat loaf was overbearing. My advice is that what you thought was sage didn't *taste* like it. I think a little more *thyme* would balance things out." From Elizabeth's narrowed gaze, Emma knew her message regarding unwanted advice had been received. Picking up the new hat from the counter, she turned it over to remove the price tag from the sweatband. "The potatoes were fine, once you got past the lumps, but the gravy was—" she frowned up at a visibly perplexed Thomas "—inconsistent."

Apparently it was not the opinion Elizabeth was looking for. She returned to the house with a muffled snort and a slam of the door, much to Emma's relief. Concentrating on keeping her hand steady when she felt anything but, she scribbled a receipt while Thomas pulled out his money clip.

"Didn't sound like you had a *gut* meal on Saturday night." The prospect seemed to please him.

"Saturday night was fine. The special was just more than I wanted."

Thomas scowled at the news and scratched his beard. Tearing the receipt duplicate from her pad, Emma pushed his copy across the counter. When he made no move to take it, she raised an eyebrow.

He rubbed the back of his neck. "What *I'd* want... What I'd like...is for us to be able to get beyond my foolishness and be friends again."

The prospect gave her a pang. His sincerity was obvious. But words could be like a nail driven into a fence post. The nail might be pulled out, but the hole remained. Cocking her head, Emma considered him. "Were we ever really friends, Thomas?"

His jaw lowered. He blinked a few times as if he couldn't understand the question. "You were at our home as much as we were over here. You and Pricilla were always together."

"*Ja*. Priscilla and I were best friends. Which

meant you and I were thrown together a lot." Her nose prickled and the backs of her eyes stung. "I miss her."

A brief spasm crossed his face. "So do I."

Emma concentrated on breathing shallowly until any threat of tears subsided before she spoke. "She was like a ray of sunshine and a soothing, quenching rain, all at the same time."

Thomas nodded. Picking up his new hat, he set it on his head. His hand dropped to stroke a finger over the tattered crown of the older one that remained on the counter. "I wish she were here now. She always knew what to do, about so many things."

"*Ja*. And tactful on her advice, for sure and certain, unlike some I know. After a conversation, you came away thinking what she'd said was your own idea in the first place."

Throat bobbing in a swallow, Thomas nodded again. His solemn eyes held hers. "Regarding your earlier question—if we weren't friends before, I'd like to be now."

The corners of Emma's mouth crept up, but it was a rueful lift. Thomas was finally looking at *her* with all the sincerity and intensity that she'd ever dreamed of. But all he wanted was to be friends. "I'd like that too."

He dipped his chin in acknowledgment, picked up his old hat and went out the door.

Emma watched through the window as he climbed into his buggy and hesitated. She furrowed her brow when he climbed back down, carrying a bag, and headed for the door. Hastily stepping away from the window, she plunked down at the sewing machine because she didn't want to look like she'd been watching him.

Setting the bag on the counter, he gave her a shadow of a smile and stepped back out the door. A moment later, she heard retreating hoofbeats. Rising from her seat at the machine, she crossed to the counter and hesitantly opened the bag. Her mouth rounding in an O, she pulled out a metal device on a walnut base. Gently, she pushed down on the lever and watched as heavy teeth clenched. She knew what it was. She knew her hands wouldn't have any issue using it to crack walnuts. What she didn't know was why he'd made it for her. It was an extraordinary gift. *Oh, Thomas. I had you safely walled away for years. But now, you besiege me from so many directions.*

Shading his eyes against the setting sun, Thomas looked out over the pasture. He couldn't blame the big horses for wanting to stay out in the pleasant spring day as long as possible, but still, it'd be nice if they'd come when he called. Just in case, he cupped his hands and hollered again. Although they all lifted their tawny heads to look at him, one by one they dropped again to graze.

Sighing, he started down the hill. They were contrary, like his neighbor.

But what had he expected? Just because he'd finally gotten through an apology last week, not only had he assumed things would automatically resume the way they'd always been, but he'd also foolishly assumed they'd get even better. That Emma would realize without him having to tell her that she should be spending time with him and not Henry, whose buggy he'd seen go by a time or two over the past few days.

But although Cilla had crossed the creek to visit Emma, there'd been no visits from the opposite direction. Not a peep. Or even a casserole dish. He'd much rather have Emma's company now and suffer his own cooking, although Cilla was getting proficient with boxed meals and canned tuna. He'd told Emma he'd wanted to be friends—it was a good starting place. It just wasn't where he wanted to finish.

At least she'd acknowledged his gift. A very nice, neighborly thank-you note had arrived in the mail. A friend would've come over and told him thanks in person, or even hollered it across the creek, instead of getting the US Postal Service and the local postmistress involved.

The Belgians raised their heads at his approach. He stroked his hand along the neck and side of the nearest gentle giant before giving it a light slap on the rump in encouragement to head to the barn. With a snort, the gelding started up the hill at a walk, which soon lengthened to a trot when he apparently remembered the grain that awaited him there. The others quickly followed suit in a rumble of heavy hooves.

Thomas glanced toward the woods and creek that divided the properties on this section, some distance from the low area where Cilla and the calf had gotten stuck. The foliage had been expanding by the day, but it was still possible to see into the depths of the timber. In a few weeks, even the first foot of woods would be dense with greenery.

Thomas's gaze wandered the shadowed midst, searching for the distinct silhouette of an alert deer looking back at him, when he caught a glimpse of something that rooted him to the spot.

Lifting a hand, he rubbed it over his heart. He'd forgotten about Priscilla's pony cart. He drifted in that direction even before he was aware he was moving. Stepping over logs and dodging saplings that'd grown significantly in the past four years, Thomas reached the two-wheeled buggy. Following a few slow breaths, he ran a hand over the seat's faded paint.

He'd made the pony cart, painted in as bright a color as allowed by the *Ordnung,* for Priscilla. She'd loved it for trips over to Emma's so she didn't have to harness the bigger horse and buggy. Their children had used it as well when they were younger, until Lena had left and the boys felt they'd outgrown a pony. So in the end, it was just Priscilla's again. When she'd died, it'd been too painful to see it in the barn. He'd pulled the cart down into the woods and sold the pony out of the district so he wouldn't see someone else in the area driving the animal.

Thomas cleared a few shrubs away to reveal more of the cart. Priscilla had always kept it so pristine. The iron frame, once a sleek black, was rusting, and the seat was considerably faded from its original cheerful color. She'd be disappointed to see it now.

He swallowed as he pulled off the hairy vines that draped over the seat. Would she be disappointed to see *him* as he was now? He supposed so. Though he was still well respected in the district, he certainly didn't interact like he had when they'd been a couple. Thomas freed one of the wheels from the undergrowth. Priscilla had been the better half of him, the one that'd drawn them into social functions. He was more reserved, held back, went when he had to. He'd rather stay at home and work or spend the evening with only her—and frequently Emma—for company.

Why did his thoughts always come back to Emma?

Clearing more brush, he worked his way around the back of the cart. His granddaughter wanted a pony. For never having been around them, she was quite comfortable with the big horses. But she wanted a pony. He had pasture for it, even an unused stall in the barn that used to hold Priscilla's Standardbred. Although the man usually dealt with bigger equines, Samuel Schrock, the local horse trader, would know where to find a pony. Thomas straightened from clearing the second wheel and ran a hand down his face to find he was smiling. Who knew what silly name Cilla would come up with for the creature?

For having been out in the weather for four years, the cart didn't look too bad. *Ja*, the iron on it was rusty, but he knew what to do with iron. The seat would need painting—that was easily done. The wheels might need to be replaced, another thing he had the tools and talent to do.

Thomas freed the shaft from the vines that entwined it and gave a strong tug. The cart rocked forward. He pulled a little more and it rolled clear of the remaining undergrowth.

Cilla would want him to clean it up. Priscilla would've wanted him to as well; she'd have been disappointed he'd abandoned it in the first place. Scratching his chin, Thomas considered the cart. *He* wanted to do it too. With a grunt, he began to drag it toward the pasture. He'd take it some place where Cilla wouldn't see while he worked on it. Like her grandmother, he wanted to surprise her with it. And maybe show someone else as well.

The needle slowed to a halt. Wincing, Emma leaned back from the sewing machine, extending and flexing the fingers of her right hand. The stiffness was encroaching.

She snorted softly. At some point, sewing hats for a living might become too difficult. Maybe that was a reason to get married. For sure and certain, there'd be many household chores to keep up with, and she would, but those didn't cause the problems that continuous sewing seemed to do. She supposed she could order in hats to sell. Other districts without access to a local hatmaker bought them from a store—clothing, fabric, farm supply—

she'd seen hats in all of them. But the margin wasn't the same. Neither would be the satisfaction. Her income wasn't that much, but still, between hers and what Elizabeth made, they managed to get by.

Emma's eyes widened. If she were to marry and leave their home, what would that do to Elizabeth's financial situation? With both of them working, it hadn't been an issue. But with her income gone, how would Elizabeth manage alone?

It was time to tell her about the letters. Emma had been doing a lot of correspondence lately, including a thank-you note sent last week to Thomas for—her gaze drifted to the nutcracker that sat on the windowsill—a gift she treasured. Of course, that wasn't what she told him in the letter, which had been very proper and cordial. Very friendly.

Friends. Is that why he'd given it to her, because they were friends? He'd obviously made it before he'd said what he said. When *had* he made it? Emma rolled her eyes. *Here I go again. Thinking I see something because I want to, not because it's really there.* But still, the thoughtful gift had raised her hopes again. That's why a thank-you note had been sent instead of telling him in person. In case she was reading too much into it, she didn't want to be rejected in person. Again. Better to not know and nourish a sliver of hope instead of determining her longing was indeed hopeless.

She shook her head at her foolishness. Why him? Thomas wasn't charming; he wasn't a smooth talker. When she'd been in her *rumspringa*, there'd been many of those in the district. Why hadn't she fallen for one of them? She'd probably still be single. They'd never really looked in her direction, and if they had, she might've done something she'd regret when charmed by their flowery speeches. At least she knew Thomas was sincere. Had she fallen for him because of his awkwardness? Whatever it was about him, Priscilla, the sweetest girl in the district, had seen it and fallen for him too.

From the growing stack of letters in her dresser, there were obviously men who wanted more from her than just friendship. Men who were willing, even eager, to court her. She needed to put her foolishness for Thomas on the shelf like one of her completed hats and focus on the others who'd indicated they wanted her. But frustratingly, the unknown one still outweighed the known many. Her gaze landed again on the nutcracker. Frowning, she leaned forward and put her foot back on the treadle.

She jumped at the jingle of the shop door. Her pulse accelerated when Cilla bounded in. Emma glanced out the window, hoping to see the buggy she hadn't heard. The yard was empty, as was the doorway behind Cilla. Her heart rate made a disappointed return to normal.

"I saw you in the window so I knew you were in here." Cilla strode over to stand by Emma's shoulder. "What'cha working on?"

"A hat." Glancing down at the almost-finished project, Emma's lips twitched at the obvious answer.

Wrinkling her nose, Cilla tugged at the tied ends of the scarf that covered her coiled hair. "I wish girls could wear hats like that."

Emma couldn't disagree. There'd been a time or two as a young girl when she'd wished the same thing. "I haven't seen you for a few days."

"I've missed you too. But I've made some new friends."

"I'm so glad for you. It's *wunderbar* to have friends."

Cilla toyed with the roll of ribbon Emma used for hat bands. "I know you haven't been over in a while, but could you come and help my grandpa? He's a mess."

Chapter Fourteen

Emma's hands paused while her heart stuttered. Thomas was indeed a mess, needing to get back to living after Priscilla's death. But Cilla's statement could mean many things. Farming was dangerous work. Blacksmithing as well. And it could just be a ploy to get the two of them together. The girl had proven she could be quite clever in her efforts.

Shifting to face her, Emma put her hands in her lap. "What do you mean?"

"He's grumpy."

Emma's tense shoulders relaxed. "That's just his normal personality."

"Well, he's particularly grumpy now. I think it has to do with the itching."

"The itching?"

"*Ja*. His arms have, like, red bubble things

on them. And his face too. It doesn't look like his normal face. He looks pretty miserable."

Emma frowned as she thought of what red bubble things on Thomas's arms and face might be. Chicken pox? That'd gone through the neighborhood when they'd been children. Thomas had endured it, as had she. Measles? Another thing they'd addressed as a youth. Shingles? Chiggers?

She furrowed her brow. "Did he say what he thought it might be?"

Cilla nodded solemnly. "Yeah. He got poisoned."

"Poisoned!"

"Yeah. When he was in the woods."

Oh, dear. While poison ivy affected most folks, Thomas was particularly susceptible. As a youngster, he'd had cases so bad that his arms had been swollen for days, which was why he was usually careful around the plant now. Emma didn't recall that he'd ever had a case this early in the year, but the oil that caused the troublesome rash was on all parts of the plant, even in winter.

Springing to her feet, she entered the house and headed for the bathroom to check what remedies she might possess. "What's he doing for it?"

Cilla trailed in her wake. "He's muttering a

lot. I know he's trying not to scratch because he mutters about that. I followed him out to his shop, and he got really cranky there."

"I can imagine. Heat makes a poison ivy rash even more inflamed. And a blacksmith shop can get pretty warm."

"It makes me sad for him. I don't know much about grandpas, but lately he's been pretty okay as one, I guess. So I came to see if you could help him. Because I don't think he'd tell anyone."

"*Nee*, he wouldn't. You say his face doesn't look normal?"

"Yeah. It's all puffy. Even under his beard."

Oh, dear. Emma snagged a few more items from the bathroom and returned to the shop. Grabbing her Be Back Later sign to hang on the door, she headed to the shed, where Cilla helped her harness Cricket. A short time later, they were crossing the bridge.

"Oh, Thomas." Emma halted as soon as she stepped over the threshold. She could understand Cilla's concern. Just seeing Thomas's swollen face and angry rash, Emma hurt for him. It was impossible to know what his reaction might be to her presence, if he could even see her with his puffy eyes. In quick strides, she crossed the floor toward where he sat, unmoving, in his chair.

The odor of apple cider vinegar hit her halfway across the room. "I won't ask how you're feeling. At least you're treating it with something. Have you showered thoroughly?" As long as the oil from the plant was on skin, it could cause problems.

"Ja." His lips barely moved amongst the angry red splotches showing above his beard.

"How about the clothes you were wearing when you might've been exposed?"

"Floor of the laundry room."

"Don't touch them, Cilla, or if you have, make sure to wash thoroughly. Poison ivy can't transfer from person to person, but the oil that causes the rash can still transfer to you from clothes. You can get it from a hoe handle that's been touched, or even the fur of your cat, if she walked through it. I'll take care of the clothes later and scrub down the room." Emma turned back to Thomas. Just a fraction of the blue eyes regarding her were visible. She gave a sympathetic shake of her head. "You know your issues with poison ivy. Leaves of three, let them be. How did you get this?" She gestured toward his blotchy red forearms, the blisters dotted like a dense forest along their insides.

Something resembling a wince crossed his face. "I was distracted."

"Must've been. Are you doing anything for

them besides the apple cider to try to dry it up? Anything else for the itch relief?"

He shook his head.

She set down her supplies. "I'll get compresses to give you some relief. But if your face swells anymore, I'm taking you to the doctor." She held up her hand at his faint denial, one she'd anticipated. "Think of it this way, Thomas. You want to get back to work as quickly as possible. They can prescribe medications for you that will give you more comfort and help you heal faster than any remedy I can provide, although I'll do the best I can. Is it anywhere beyond your face and forearms?"

"Nee." Even as he spoke, he raised a hand to scratch at the center of his chest.

"Uh-uh." Impulsively, she leaned over to catch it. To her surprise, and instantly pounding heart rate, instead of returning his hand to the chair's armrest, he turned it over and gently clasped her own. Emma couldn't move. Couldn't look beyond the glimpse of his blue eyes. Couldn't regret that he could probably feel her rapid pulse beating where his thumb rested against her wrist.

"Will it ever go down?"

Abruptly straightening, Emma released her grip as she turned at Cilla's question. Although it couldn't have lasted that long, the moments stretched as his calloused fingers slid slowly along the length of hers. She didn't take a full breath until his hand dropped to the chair.

Licking her suddenly dry lips, Emma cupped her hand at her side, the skin humming from fingertip to wrist. Go down? Not for a while. Neither her heart rate nor her chronic hopes would diminish, although she knew Cilla had been referring to Thomas's face.

"Ja." The response was too faint to be heard. She cleared her throat and tried again. *"Ja.* I'll get those cool compresses, and we'll get calamine lotion on. I also brought some over-the-counter antihistamines." She braced herself to meet his gaze again. "You're not allergic, are you?"

He shook his head, his eyes never leaving hers. She swallowed at the sensation that even a fraction of their blue depths sent through her. "If we can't get you some comfort with the compresses, I'll set up an oatmeal or baking soda bath." Tearing her gaze away, she wrinkled her nose. "And try rubbing alcohol afterward instead of the apple cider vinegar to dry out the rash. The smell isn't as strong."

Emma hastened to the kitchen where she hoped to find some clean dish towels to wet for compresses. She lifted the hand that'd clasped his to her heated cheek. Cool compresses that she might need to use on own her flushed face.

* * *

Thomas concentrated his view on Emma working in the kitchen, a needed distraction to keep from scratching. He'd had enough poison ivy rashes to know if he scratched too much, it could lead to broken skin and risks of infection. And, however much he might be suffering right now, the rash would go away in two to three weeks.

He knew where he'd been exposed. The vines he'd unthinkingly pulled from the cart the other day had been poison ivy. He just hadn't been thinking to see it this early in the spring. *Ach*, he hadn't been thinking of much else but Emma, and yesterday, the cart. Today, he was just thinking of Emma.

She'd kept talking about giving him comfort. With a soft exhale and release of the tension that'd pervaded him since he'd first recognized the rash, he settled into his chair. She'd given him more comfort than she could've imagined, just by being here. Just by being Emma. If a poison ivy rash was what it took to get her over here, it was worth wallowing in the stuff—Thomas cringed as he focused on not scratching a particularly itchy spot on his arm—maybe.

He wished he didn't look like an overinflated balloon. Lifting a corner of his mouth against the stiffness of his cheek, Thomas sniffed. Cider wasn't what he'd smelled when she'd leaned in. Amish women didn't wear perfume, so it must've been shampoo or soap? Or just the essence of Emma. A clean, bright, genuine scent. One he'd like to have permeate his senses, his home. And his life.

He liked seeing her bustling about the house. Thomas braced for the pang he'd always felt, that it was Priscilla's home too, but as the seconds ticked by and only the pleasure of hearing Emma opening drawers and running water in the kitchen remained, he relaxed again.

When, with gentle fingers, she laid the cool, wet compress over his swollen face a short while later, Thomas couldn't see through the cloth, so he'd just closed his eyes and…felt. He felt good. He felt peaceful. He felt content. If it wasn't for the agitation in his face and arms, he felt the best he had since Priscilla was gone. He hadn't realized how much he'd missed a woman's touch. *Be honest with yourself, Thomas. Not just a woman's touch. Emma's touch.*

Just Emma's touch.

Flexing his fingers, he swallowed carefully, hoping she wouldn't notice the bob of his throat while she attended to him.

"Am I hurting you?" Her voice was soft.

Gentle. He knew she had that side of her although it'd never been directed at him, but often was toward those he'd held close. Like he wanted to hold her close. But Emma also had a steel side and a fun side. He'd seen those over the years. He appreciated all aspects of her. He respected all aspects. He…he swallowed again. He *loved* all aspects. Even with his bloated features, Thomas was thankful for the compress that additionally concealed his expression.

How could he love Emma when he swore he'd always love Priscilla? He'd loved her from the first moment he'd noticed her as a petite six-year-old on the first day she'd come to school. She'd been holding Emma's hand as they'd tentatively entered the schoolhouse door. And now, the one he wanted to hold his hand, the one who held his heart, was Emma, his neighbor, who'd always been there, even when he hadn't really seen her.

Although frustration at not being in his shop and the desire to scratch continually plagued him, it was a wonderful afternoon. Every fifteen to thirty minutes Emma would replace the compresses, being quiet as she did so, seeming not to need much from him in response, which suited Thomas perfectly.

He heard talk in the kitchen as Emma

coached Cilla on making something for supper, the aroma of which floated to him later. When he sat down to supper with them, Thomas used his silent prayer before eating as one of thanks, and of entreaty that he not stumble on the journey of making this wonderful temporary situation into a permanent one.

Chapter Fifteen

Thomas pushed back the brim of his hat and wiped his sweaty forehead with his wrist, which thankfully had finally cleared from the angry rash. What hadn't cleared in the past few weeks was his workload. The days he'd missed in the shop in the early part of his affliction, and the shortened days as the irritation had slowly improved, were evident in his customer backlog.

He returned the alloy he'd been drawing down to the fire to reheat, watching the metal begin to glow with a frown. A coworker could've picked up the slack while he was out. Though there wasn't enough work for all of them, regrettably, not one of his sons were interested in coming back to join him. They seemed quite happy in Shipshe. The two older boys had married girls from there. Thomas had taken the bus to attend the weddings, missing Priscilla with every mile to and from Indiana. She would've loved to have seen them married.

His gaze strayed to the envelope on the bench, one with a Shipshewana address, and his frown deepened. His oldest son had responded to the letter Thomas had written him some time ago—one he'd since forgotten. Eager to hear how his *kinner* were doing, he'd opened the correspondence with anticipation. Upon scanning the single page, he'd tapped the letter against his thigh and eyed his forge for the missive's disposal before returning it to the envelope with a sigh and setting it on the bench. The letter had been brief and easily memorized in a single reading.

Originally his son didn't think they'd have a place for Cilla, but since their family would be expanding, a helping hand would be useful. Beyond that, he had an eye on a piece of property that was big enough to grow extra produce. When the girl finished school in a few years, her help in the garden would be an asset. As the *boppeli* wouldn't arrive for a few months, they didn't need her for a while, but if it was a factor, Thomas could send her along at his convenience. Just let them know when to pick her up at the bus stop.

Pulling the metal from the fire, Thomas set

it back on his anvil to give it a mighty *thwack* with his hammer. He didn't want to send Cilla along at his convenience. He smacked the glowing rod again. He didn't want to send her along...ever. *Thwack!* He'd gotten used to having her around. Used to odd names assigned to his livestock, startling observations, exuberant barn help, interesting food at his table and spontaneous, affectionate hugs.

Where had his *sohn* learned to be so cold? Certainly not from their *mamm*. From him then? Had he always been that aloof? Not with Priscilla, but with his children? Is that why they'd all left? Turning the metal with his tongs, Thomas pounded it into a longer, thinner shape. He'd emulated behavior he'd witnessed from his father. Had Priscilla ever called him on it? Or had she just picked up the slack as best as she could in parenting their children? Growing up, his father had ruled the family. But lately he was seeing marriages in the community that were partnerships, like Ruth and Malachi Schrock, Rachel and Ben Raber and the younger Weavers.

He'd like to think he'd had that with Priscilla, but he *knew* he could have that kind of relationship with Emma. The past few weeks had been *wunderbar*. At first, Emma had come over every day as he got over the worst of his reaction. She'd tend to him, provide Cilla another cooking or baking lesson and stay for supper. He'd improved—almost to his regret—and her visits had dropped to every other day. But in those two weeks, they'd almost become a family.

If they were a real one, together he and Emma could raise Cilla. Thomas's heart started pounding harder than his weighted hammer on the metal. If he married Emma, they could provide a home for his granddaughter so there'd be no need for her to leave to be a baby minder and produce picker for his son. Cilla would have a *gut* home right here, *if* he married Emma.

Scowling at the metal which he'd pounded into a longer shape than he needed, Thomas returned it to the fire. *Oh, Thomas, admit it. You want to marry Emma because you want her. Not just as a reason to provide a home for Cilla.* He dropped onto the stool by his workbench.

But would that be enough for Emma? While he wanted her just because she was, well, Emma, she might need a better reason to want to marry him.

She liked Cilla. They got along well. Cilla would certainly be happy with the arrangement. *Ja*, Emma would probably say yes, *if* she thought the reason was for Cilla. He smiled. But it wouldn't be. Not entirely.

Thomas blinked a few moments later at finding himself staring at his array of punches that lined the wall, daydreaming like a lovesick *youngie*. He jumped up from the stool. *Ja*, he'd ask Emma to marry him, as soon as possible, before Henry Troyer beat him to it.

The opportunity came sooner than he'd expected. He'd barely beaten the metal back into shape when he heard voices at the open door of the shop. A moment later, Cilla, followed by Emma, stepped inside.

She smiled at him. "How're you feeling today?"

"Better." Thomas fought a return smile. He couldn't tell her how he really felt. That she made him glow like the coals in his forge. That seeing her walk in his door was like the sun coming up for the second time that day.

Remembering what he'd determined to ask her, Thomas felt like his anvil had dropped into his belly. This would be as good a time as any. It had the benefit of being in his shop, where he felt more comfortable. Priscilla had seldom been in here, so significant new memories seemed more comfortable alongside precious, previous ones. Rubbing the back of his neck, he watched as Cilla wandered about the shop. He just had a little more company than seemed appropriate for the moment. He cleared his throat to get his granddaughter's attention.

"Glad to hear it." Emma sounded like she actually was. Did that mean she was relieved not to have to come over so much anymore? Thomas hoped not.

Moments ticked by. "Heat not bothering what's left of the rash?" Emma's voice, a little less confident, broke the silence.

"Nee." Thomas stared hard at Cilla, willing her to look up from her investigation of the vices and clamps he used to hold his projects. Having no success, he glanced at Emma to see her wring her hands and look toward the door as if she might leave.

Beginning to panic, he cleared his throat again. "Cilla, why don't you go play with your kitten?"

Cilla lifted one of the smaller claps as if to weigh it in her hand. "She's sleeping."

Thomas crossed his arms over his chest. "How about the calf, Barbie."

The girl finally looked over. "It's Bambi. And you let her and Faline into the back pasture this morning." She cocked her head at him. "Don't you remember? Or does the poison ivy stuff affect your brain as well as your skin?"

"Hmm, how about going in and making some lemonade for us?"

At the suggestion, Emma interjected. "That sounds good, but I really need to be going. I just stopped by to see how you were doing."

He was going to lose his opportunity, and who knew when he'd get another. How much time did it take to propose? It'd been so long since he'd done so. "I'll walk you to your buggy."

Emma's cheeks flushed. Was it the heat of his shop, or had they grown rosy at his offer? The possibility gave a spring to his step as he followed her out the door. A spring that wilted when Cilla moseyed out right on their heels.

"Um, would you mind getting the feed out for the Belgians?"

His granddaughter squinted at the height of the sun. "Isn't it a little early?"

It was, but Thomas was running out of both suggestions and distance toward the buggy. He and Emma were strolling side by side, arms almost brushing. Thomas was tempted to reach for her hand, just to see what she would do. Instead, he rubbed his perspiring palms down his pant legs. Maybe if they lingered at the buggy a bit, Cilla would wander off like she normally did.

Apparently unimpressed by their ambling pace, his granddaughter dodged around them to skip to the buggy and peer into the open door.

"What're all those? Are you helping deliver the mail or something? Or are they birthday cards? Is your birthday coming up?"

The change in Emma was instantaneous. It was like someone plugged her into a generator. She went from sauntering to surging toward the buggy herself. Curious, Thomas increased his speed as well. He looked through the door as Emma hastily untied her mare. There was indeed a collection of letters on the buggy's seat, one that Cilla was currently fingering through. Thomas stiffened when he noticed an address in another district where he'd delivered a project. The man had been a widower with a prosperous farm. He quickly scanned the other addresses, ones penned in what appeared to be masculine handwriting.

Emma blocked their view as she scrambled into the buggy. Plopping onto the seat, she flipped her skirt over the bundle of letters. "*Nee.* Not my birthday. Just a little correspondence. So glad you're doing better. *Mach's gut.*"

Returning her hasty farewell, Thomas stepped back before she could run over his foot. His gaze narrowed as it followed her buggy down the lane. It was a *lot* of correspondence. All addressed to Emma, whose cheeks had gone from slightly rosy to brilliant red before she raced away. Why?

"You still want some lemonade?"

Thomas shook his head. He and Cilla needed to work out their timing if he was going to get a proposal offered. He watched as Emma turned onto the road and her horse sprang into a trot. Especially if Henry wasn't his only competition.

Emma was a quarter mile down the road before the breeze coming through the open door finally cooled her cheeks. She'd forgotten about the letters, having picked them up from the mailbox when she'd left home this morning. As discovering another handful when she opened the door no longer gave her the shock and thrill it initially had, she'd just tossed the arrivals onto the seat to be read later. She hadn't even checked to see if there were any new return addresses other than the ten with whom she'd already been corresponding. Scooting them out from under her, she glanced with a frown at the assorted envelopes.

Susannah had been modest about her role, but she'd certainly exceeded any expectations Emma ever had for a matchmaker. With all the letters from far-flung areas that'd shown up in her mailbox, Emma had started scanning their weekly newspaper, *The Budget*, just to ensure Susannah hadn't placed some advertisement about her in them.

Although she'd never anticipated it, Emma now understood what Sarah Raber had been talking about. She didn't really like walking in a forest. All she wanted was one tree. What was she going to do with all this extra timber?

Initially enchanted and enjoying the boost to her confidence, she'd written to them. They seemed like nice men—some funny, some lonely, all seemingly sincere. Several had been flatteringly quick to respond. Although she hadn't encouraged it, she could tell a few might soon pose a question she wasn't sure she'd have an answer for.

Did she really want to get married?

Did she really want to change her life so completely? Move out of her district, out of her comfortable home, her comfortable life? *Ja*, she was lonely, but only for a special someone's companionship. Though Priscilla was gone, she still had *gut* friendships, *gut* fellowship in her community, satisfaction in her work for as long as she could do it and a *gut* relationship with her sister, even when they didn't always see eye to eye. It wasn't the life she'd expected, it wasn't one she'd dreamed of, but still, it was a *gut* one. Maybe, as it said in the *Biewel*, she'd learned to be content. Could she continue to be, in an unknown life, one where there'd be gains in a culture organized to walk by twos, but also freedoms—ones she had as a single woman determining her own direction—lost.

Emma poked through the stack of letters beside her, unearthing a few new return addresses as well as some recognized ones, before directing her attention to the road ahead. She sighed, her shoulders drooping.

She wanted a tree. Just one. These past few weeks with Thomas and Cilla had been the highlight of her year, the highlight of her decade. Thomas had looked at her a time or two—once the swelling had gone down and she could fully see his eyes—in such a way that she'd hoped, that she'd allowed herself to dream, that he finally saw her as she saw him. As a possibility, a partner. A future.

There'd been no real need for her to stop on her way back from town; she'd become so content seeing Thomas on a regular basis, she'd driven there automatically. But today, he'd acted strange, distracted, even abrupt. After expecting something different, it'd unsettled her. And then Cilla had noticed the letters and Emma, flustered, couldn't get down the lane fast enough.

Stopping Cricket next to the house, she gathered the letters and a few bags of groceries from the back of the buggy. Entering the house, she set the bags on the counter, turned to put the letters in her room and ran right into Elizabeth.

"Anything need putting away?" Her sister nodded toward the mail in Emma's hand. "Besides those?"

The envelopes felt like they were burning in her palm. "Some sour cream. And grapes were on sale."

"You're going to marry one of them and leave, aren't you?"

Emma crossed her arms over her chest, tucking the letters along her side. This wasn't the way she'd wanted to tell Elizabeth.

"You think I haven't noticed all the correspondence you've been doing? Besides, Karen eats at the Dew Drop every day and mentioned all the mail you've been receiving. And sending."

Emma wasn't surprised. The local postmistress probably read the backs of the postcards that came through their small community. "Nobody has asked."

"I was asked once. Moses asked me. I couldn't say yes fast enough. Then he told me he was planning on leaving with his family when they moved back to Ohio. He figured we'd join them as soon as we married. It was right after *Daed* lost his foot to the gangrene. I couldn't leave you alone to take care of him. Not with more issues possible due to his diabetes." Elizabeth fished the sour cream and grapes from one of the bags and put them in the refrigerator before turning back to where Emma, wide-eyed, stood frozen by the counter.

Her stomach twisted as she recalled the relief she'd felt when her sister's relationship, for reasons unknown, had broken off. She couldn't imagine not having Elizabeth by her side during those awful months, when they'd seemingly lost their father little by little until finally, he'd given up. And then, when it'd just been the two of them, she couldn't imagine not having had her sister's company.

"So I broke it off. To stay here with family who needed me. And he left with his." Elizabeth's lip lifted in a half smile, but it was a trembling one. "After *Daed* was gone, I heard from his sister that Moses married a girl from there."

She nodded again to the letters that'd drifted into view from Emma's now lax fingers. "You do what you want. I'm just telling you what I decided when I had the choice." Turning, Elizabeth retreated down the hallway. Emma heard her door quietly shut a moment later.

With shaking fingers, she laid the letters on the counter. No one had asked. But if they did, did she really have a choice on what her answer should be?

Chapter Sixteen

Even after several brushings, the chestnut pony with its flaxen mane and tail still looked like a puffed-up dandelion. Thomas's lips twitched as, under his careful eye, Cilla turned the prancing pony into the lane. He was hoping to have the animal looking sleek for the first time Emma saw the little rig, but he didn't blame the pony for keeping most of its winter coat. The weather was about as twitchy as he was, with an unpredictable outlook.

He wanted to make this trip before the rain settled in. Even if they didn't get a downpour here, if it rained upstream, the creek could still flood the bridge, leaving him on one side with Emma and all her letters on the other. There were other options than this bridge to reach her place, but they were miles out of the way and would make a simple neighborly visit less... plausible.

When they pulled up the lane, Emma exited the shop door, her eyes as wide as her smile as she came out to meet them. The questioning glance thrown at Thomas revealed she recognized the cart, one he'd worked late evenings to finish in the week since she'd dashed down the lane with all her letters.

"What a lovely surprise!" Her face reflected the sincerity of her words. Thomas just hoped she felt the same when he said what he hoped to say today.

Cilla drew the rig to a rocking halt beside her.

"You're handling that pony like you've been doing it all your life."

"I practiced a lot yesterday. Would you like to go for a drive?" At Cilla's question, Emma's cheeks grew pink as she glanced dubiously from Thomas to the cart's narrow seat.

There wasn't room for three. Thomas promptly climbed down. Emma liked Cilla. Maybe a ride together would make her more receptive to his pending suggestion.

Emma worried her lower lip. "I guess that sounds all right." She quickly climbed in on his side of the buggy before he could assist her.

As she did so, Cilla scrambled out on her side. "My arms are tired. I'm not used to holding them out," she mimicked extending her arms like she was driving. Emma immediately moved to get down from the cart. "No, please stay put. My *grossdaddi* will take you. I'm improving, but he's a better driver, for now at least. I'll just stay here in case someone comes to the shop."

From his side of the pony, Thomas blinked at his *kinskind*. Although tempted, he hadn't mentioned his intentions regarding Emma to his granddaughter, figuring two heads weren't better than one on the topic when one was still under the age of twelve. But maybe he'd been wrong. With a sweet smile, Cilla held up the reins in her hands. The pony stomped one of his feet as if to say, *Make up your mind*.

A moment later, Thomas's sweaty palms wrapped around the leather. The two-wheeled cart creaked as, with a hard swallow, he stepped in. Any deep breath he took would brush his shoulder against Emma's. Therefore, he kept his breathing as shallow as possible as he wheeled the pony back down the lane, his heart thumping faster than the tattoo of the chestnut's hooves on the gravel.

Now what? This was obviously the moment. He risked a glance at Emma's profile. She was staring ahead, her *kapp* covering the bountiful hair that'd first caught his attention, its white ribbons flowing behind her slender neck as the pony trotted along. A neck that bobbed in a hard swallow, like his. Was she nervous too? That was good, wasn't it?

At the notion, some tension eased from his shoulders. Perversely, it felt right for this moment to occur in Priscilla's cart. Priscilla had loved her friend and would've loved her granddaughter, so anything bringing them together would've surely had her approval. The solid seat beneath him and the smoothly spinning wheels of something she'd treasured reminded him that saying yes to possibilities with Emma didn't mean he was saying no to the love and respect he had for his first wife. It was almost as if Priscilla was patting his shoulder and saying, "It's time." And it was. A peace and hope settled over him, accompanied by an eagerness for a future with the woman beside him.

If he didn't blow this important moment.

His pulse surged like it was racing the pony. Did women in their forties want romance like ones in their teens and twenties did? Probably. Thomas frowned. He hadn't done romance well when he'd been a *youngie*. Those letters from other men could've contained all sorts of sentimental notions. What if his ordinary words fell far short? His foot started tapping against the floor of the cart. Emma glanced down at the bouncing knee beside her. The pony's fuzzy ears flicked back at the disturbing sound.

Should he start by mentioning Cilla? Or by proposing? Which would be more likely to receive a positive response? Thomas put his hand on his knee to halt its jittering.

"I was surprised to see the cart again. I think she'd be happy to have it restored." Emma gingerly breached the silence.

Thomas didn't need to ask who *she* was. Maybe it was a sign. "It's a *gut* way to teach Cilla how to drive." There was the opening. He cleared his throat. "I received a letter from Emmanuel the other day."

Brightening, Emma turned toward him. "That's wonderful. How are he and your other sons doing?"

"He said if I want to send Cilla to Shipshe, he could use her help, as his family is expanding and so is his garden."

Her face immediately fell. "Oh, Thomas. You two are doing so well together. She doesn't need another change in her life right now. You can't let her go."

Thomas took a deep breath. "I know. So will you marry me?"

When she stiffened beside him, he cringed. For sure and certain, if he'd been trying, he couldn't have come up with a less romantic proposal. His foot started bouncing again. "I mean, if we were to be married, it'd be like she had a family here already."

"Oh, Thomas." Emma shook her head sadly. "She already has a family. With you. Cilla and you have become a family."

His heart seesawed between the thrill that it might be so, and the prospect that Emma was going to say no to the only reason she might have to accept his proposal. The prospect for no seemed weightier. All the moisture in his mouth seemed to have hightailed it to his forehead.

"You two get along well. A woman's influence would help her. It still might be…reasonable to get married." Widening his eyes at his stilted words, Thomas felt as dense as the rocks that lined the creek they were passing.

"It might." Emma's words were quiet.

Thomas turned the pony around on the road, his stomach feeling like one of the rocks had somehow taken lodging there. A very short trip might be a good idea right about now. He'd rather walk across his forge barefoot than drive along with an embarrassed Emma after she'd turned down his proposal. He forced out what he hoped was a casual, "So?"

She looked like she'd just consumed something that she wasn't sure would agree with her. "Thank you for asking. I…need to think about it."

He gave a jerky nod. *Ach*, at least it wasn't a flat-out no. Afraid to say more in case it changed to one, Thomas urged the pony faster. Maybe he should've had Cilla do the proposing for him. She couldn't have done a worse job.

Emma's heart was hammering. After her discussion with Elizabeth, she'd almost determined to live out her life in its lonely, though comfortable, state. She'd even sent out a few letters ending some of her correspondences.

But this was Thomas, whom she'd loved forever. The word no just wouldn't form on her lips. She wanted to hug the awkward proposal to her heart. She wanted to burst out with a yes so enthusiastic that it startled the pony and even more so, Thomas.

Barely containing herself, she snuck a look at her companion. His profile was as frozen as the nearby creek in subzero temperatures. He didn't look like someone thrilled at the prospect of becoming a bridegroom. So why was he asking her? Was it because of Cilla and nothing else? Or had he discovered it was nice having someone take care of him again? Emma clasped her hands in her lap. She could do that. She could take good care of him. And Cilla. She'd love to do so.

The pony cut the corner into the lane, one

wheel bouncing precariously close to the ditch. Emma's stomach swooped like they'd actually dipped in. Would he expect her to be just like Priscilla? Was Thomas really ready to have room in his heart for anyone else? Was he ready to have room for her, specifically?

Emma gently massaged the tender knuckles in her hand and worked her way up a wrist that ached with the pending rain. Could she settle for being just Thomas's housekeeper, cook, caretaker—a poor substitute for his much-loved wife? Or would it be better to keep her own heart safe and behind its walls, as she'd done for so long?

Cilla was obviously startled at how soon they'd arrived back at the house and even more so at how quickly she and her grandfather were heading down the lane again behind the pony's flaxen tail.

Thomas's response to her solemn "I'll let you know" was an equally solemn nod. And she would, as soon as her thoughts stopped buzzing like bees in a hive and she knew what that response would be.

They were still buzzing two days later. She'd waited all her life for him. He could wait a few days for her.

She'd decide yes, then her gaze would rest

on Elizabeth before her sister left for work and she'd decide no. Then she'd consider that if Thomas was ready to marry again and she'd turned him down, what if he married someone else in the community, someone who wasn't her best friend whom she'd always known would cherish him as she loved them both? Imagining Thomas married to someone other than Priscilla made her slightly ill.

Then there was Cilla, whom she already loved and the feeling seemed to be mutual. Would anyone else Thomas might eventually choose care for his granddaughter like she did? So then she'd decide yes, but what if—

The exterior shop door opened and Elizabeth stepped inside, shaking the rain off her black umbrella. Emma swiveled on her seat at the sewing machine, away from the hat she'd probably never be able to sell due to all the distracted mistakes she'd been making. Her breath escaped in a burst at the sight of the envelopes in her sister's hand.

Elizabeth leaned the closed umbrella against the wall. "Picked up the mail. Seems it's been a while since I've done so."

Emma remained seated. Days ago, she might've lunged from her chair to get the letters. She didn't even flinch when Elizabeth flipped through the envelopes to pull one to the front of the bundle.

"Is this why you've been dithering around the past few days?"

"*Nee*. Although it was exciting to receive them and communicate with them, I've decided that, though I was dreaming of a change, if I were to marry at all, it wouldn't be to anyone outside of the community."

"Henry Troyer then?" Elizabeth eyed her shrewdly.

With a rueful smile, Emma shook her head. "Henry's a *gut* man, but he's more like a brother that we never had."

Elizabeth grunted. "What about Thomas?"

Leaning an elbow on her sewing machine table, Emma cupped a flushed cheek in her hand. "Thomas asked me to marry him the other day."

"So." Elizabeth tapped the envelopes against her side. "When's the wedding?"

"I told him I'd have to think about it."

"Why?"

"I think he only wants to marry me because of Cilla. To give her a more solid home life."

"Huh. From what I've heard of the girl, she can handle just about any circumstances pretty well. You've wanted him for years. When he asked, why didn't you jump on him like a hen on a bug?"

Emma crossed her arms over her chest with a deep sigh. "I was afraid he'd compare me to Priscilla."

"Priscilla's been gone for years. Thomas isn't a fool. He knows you're not his first wife. The reason to marry him is that you love him. Do you?"

"Ja."

"Then do it."

"What about you?"

Elizabeth's lips twisted at the question. She looked about the shop for a moment before her blue eyes met Emma's identical ones.

"I've done some dithering too. I'm sorry about the other day. I…uh… I'd thought Moses would come back for me. I mean, he would've if he'd really loved me. So I guess I made the right choice in calling it off. But that doesn't mean you should do the same. I was envious, which is wrong, and I'll…miss you." Dropping her gaze, she toed the dripping umbrella, scattering drops of water over the linoleum. "If you're going to marry anyone and leave this house, marry Thomas. At least you'll only be across the creek. You could probably keep the store, and I'd gain a grandniece."

When she looked up, she wore a small smile.

"Besides, I'll be spending a bit more time at work. Selling the restaurant has taken longer than the *Englisch* owners thought, and they want to move closer to family. They've asked me to take over some of the management role. It comes with a pay raise."

She extended the letters toward Emma. "I don't know if it'll help or hurt in your decision, but the postmistress is as thorough as she is snoopy."

Brow lowered in confusion, Emma took the envelopes. Glancing at the front one, she immediately rose to her feet.

"The man doesn't say much. Maybe he writes better than he talks. I'm surprised he could find an available stamp in his house. But I doubt he'd send a letter to withdraw a proposal. Best put him out of his misery and give him an answer."

The other letters tumbled to the floor as Emma tore open Thomas's letter. Upon scanning the single page, she pressed it against her heart.

Elizabeth gestured to the mail at Emma's feet. "I take it you're not interested in those anymore?"

"*Nee*. Would you like them?"

"What? You're offering me your hand-me-downs? That's a first." Elizabeth's smile was wry. "Maybe it's about time. But not for a man.

I've gotten too used to running things my own way by now."

Stooping, Emma quickly gathered up the other letters. "Speaking of running, I have someplace I need to go."

Elizabeth gave a surprised *oof* at Emma's tight hug. Releasing her, Emma headed for the connecting door to the house with Elizabeth's bemused warning trailing after her. "It's raining out there."

"I don't care. Even if the bridge was underwater, I'd float across it somehow."

Chapter Seventeen

Cricket didn't think much of the impromptu trip out into the rain. As she trotted across the bridge, the mare snorted and warily eyed the water that licked at the edge of the concrete bridge on one side and gushed out of the culverts into the swollen creek on the other. The normally docile stream had become a raging flood with the recent rains.

Maybe the horse had more sense than she did. To make such a life-changing decision based on a few written words? Very few, in fact. To Elizabeth's speculation, Thomas *didn't* write any better than he talked, but the simple words on the page beside her—"I didn't ask just for Cilla. It was for me too."—and the fact that he'd written them, tipped the scale in his favor.

Oh, Emma. Who do you think you're fooling? You wanted to say yes all along. Still, her stomach was knotted more than the braided straw used in her hats.

By the time she pulled up to his house, her heartbeat was racing to the cadence of the raindrops against her buggy. The drumming of both slowed as she lingered on the seat, gathering courage. With a deep sigh, she finally climbed down. By the time she reached the refuge of the porch, her dress was more wet than dry. Wiping water from her face, Emma's hand drifted to a stop when she saw Thomas striding from the direction of his shop.

Do I look as anxious as he does? Schooling her face to calmness, she tried out a smile. Thomas offered a tentative one himself and sped up, almost walking through one of the mud puddles that dotted the yard in the process. Emma's smile blossomed to a grin as he jumped at the last minute to avoid it. Thomas might not be the most handsome or wealthiest man in the state or even the district, but he was finally going to be hers. This one tree was better than a hundred-acre forest.

Before he reached the steps, the door behind her opened.

"Are you just going to stay out here on the porch?"

She might. Or maybe even stand out in the rain with her arms raised in jubilation. Instead, Emma turned to share her smile with a bemused Cilla, who looked quite Amish in a bright blue dress and neatly arranged hair. *It wasn't just for Cilla*, his words had said, but there was much she had done and would love to do for the girl. *It was for me too.* Just as she longed to do for the girl's grandfather.

Emma felt more than saw Thomas enter the house right behind her. A cool breeze followed them in, rising goose bumps on her damp skin. She resisted the urge to hug herself against the chill. Hopefully, soon Thomas's arms would wrap about her when she accepted his proposal. It was a moment she'd dreamed of all her life.

Thomas had almost sat down on top of his forge when he'd glanced out the window to see Emma's buggy pulling into the yard. She was here. She was finally here. It'd seemed like an eternity since she'd told him she'd think about his proposal. Although as a blacksmith, Thomas knew patience was required in creating a desired end, patience had been far from his mind since he'd asked his question. Which was why he'd come home that day and turned the house upside down under Cilla's curious eye to finally find a blank sheet of paper and envelope to send Emma a letter, joining the rest of the mature single Amish male population east of the Mississippi River. For an hour, he deliberated over the right words to say, the ones in his heart that would encourage her to be his wife, only to quickly jot something down and slap it into the envelope when he saw the mailman coming down the road.

And now she was here. And smiling. She wouldn't be smiling if she was going to turn him down, would she?

Now what should he do? A good start would probably be closing the door. Doing so, Thomas caught sight of a very intrigued Cilla. His smile wilted a degree, realizing he'd have an audience for this happy occasion. *Ach*, he could hardly suggest she go out into the rain on some errand. Besides, she'd be as thrilled as he was. Almost, he amended, taking a deep breath to control his runaway pulse. Still, just a moment would be nice...

"How about getting a towel to dry us off a bit, Cilla?"

"Ja." Winking at him, she promptly disappeared down the hall with Thomas staring after her. His attention whipped back when Emma cleared her throat.

"I got your letter." Her eyes were shining, her cheeks pink. She was beautiful.

Thomas hooked his thumbs into his suspenders, both for something to hold on to and to keep from reaching for her.

"*Ja*, Thomas. I will marry you."

His thumbs quickly slipped from his suspenders as his arms slid around her petite form. She was warm, vital and precious in his embrace. Like coming home to all the comforts you'd dreamed of after a long bitter night out. Closing his eyes, Thomas slowly exhaled a blend of joy and relief. He'd only ever been this happy when Priscilla had agreed to share his life.

"You've made me so happy, Priscilla."

Thomas blinked his eyes open. The warm, yielding figure in his arms was stiffening like the water in the creek at the onslaught of winter. Emma's arms lifted from around his neck before pulling away completely. As she leaned from him, he reluctantly released his hold of her now rigid back. She edged farther away. The distance to her ashen face seemed much more than the inches that separated them.

Her words were low, but they easily penetrated his hearing, his heart. "I'm a fool to think I could ever make you happy. I'm not Priscilla. I never will be. I thought I could… but I…" Her voice hitched. "I can't marry you. I'd rather continue to be a 'leftover blessing' than settle for being a poor imitation."

Before he could react, Emma darted out the door to leave him staring after her.

What had happened?

"You called her Priscilla."

He turned to see Cilla standing in the hallway, strangling the two towels she held.

"I did?" His jaw sagged as dismay slammed through him. "Oh, no. I didn't mean to..."

"Doesn't matter. Now she's gone, and she'll never want to be a part of our family. You blew it, Grandpa."

Thomas staggered over to his chair. He didn't even make it into the seat, just sagged to perch on one of the arms.

Striding over, Cilla dropped the towels into his lap. "You both kept talking about my grandma. I'll never know her, but I know Emma, and knowing her, I know I'd like my grandma 'cause she was smart enough to have Emma as her best friend. I'm sure Grandma Priscilla was great, but I can't imagine anyone being more wonderful than Emma would be as a grandma. I wanted that." She shook her head. "Now because of the one, I'll never have the other."

Thomas shoved his hands into his hair, knocking his hat askew. "*Nee.* This was my fault only. Whatever I've—" he inhaled a shaky breath "—done here, her relationship with you won't change."

"It won't be the one I wanted. The one I've been working for. I've got to…"

Her last word was muffled as she went out the door. Thomas focused on her first ones. Ones that echoed in his heart, his soul. He'd never have the relationship he wanted with Emma now. As Cilla had said, he blew it. That must've been what her last word was. Cry. Something he was tempted to do. His lips twisted. Too bad he didn't have a cat like Cilla did to hold during the dark times.

He hung his head. Now he wouldn't have Emma to hold during dark times, as well as bright ones and all the ones in between. Those few moments when she'd been in his arms were all he could've hoped for. And he'd responded with the name that'd previously defined joy for him. Because of his foolishness, those few moments with Emma were all he'd have. Now his hopes, his life, seemed as frayed as the faded towels in his lap.

He didn't blame her for turning him down. What woman wants to be called by another woman's name when she's in a man's arms?

Emma gave Cricket enough rein to do as she wished; the mare knew the way home and would head for the barn in the rain. Besides, Emma couldn't see anything past her tears anyway. When she felt the buggy slow, she dashed a hand across her eyes and over her cheeks. Sniffing, she peered past the rain drizzling down the glass to realize they were descending to the bridge. Cricket's head was up, her steps hesitant as she stepped onto concrete surrounded by roaring, swirling water.

At least her humiliation had her heading home in time to cross the bridge before the water did. But it was close. If she'd left much later, she'd have had to pass back by Thomas's place to get home another way. She didn't want to risk any possibility of seeing him again, at least not yet. Emma's breath hitched. She'd have to face him at church tomorrow. Unless she could convince Elizabeth she was ill, which shouldn't be difficult, because she certainly looked it.

In this small community, she couldn't hide from him forever. She'd see him soon and often at community functions and eventually think of what might've been. And what was. She'd always been second in her life. Secondhand, second best, second-rate. She'd wanted to be first with her husband. But for Thomas, she'd been so subordinate in his mind that he couldn't even recall her name when he'd held her in his arms.

For just a moment, Emma had been tempted. Tempted to hold on to Thomas, physically and emotionally. So hungry for a relationship with him that she'd been willing to try to step into her deceased best friend's perfect shoes. But she couldn't step into her name. She had her own. And if he couldn't see that… She scrubbed more tears from her face.

The buggy lurched. Emma grabbed at the lines when Cricket shied as a large branch slammed into the concrete. Spinning in the roiling water, it jerked like a pole with a large fish on the end before being swallowed by one of the culverts at the far end of the bridge.

For a heart-stopping moment, it seemed the spooked mare was going to leap from the bridge. As she urged the horse over the slippery concrete, Emma glanced up the swollen creek in case more debris was rushing toward them. Amidst the turbulent brown water, she caught sight of a splash of unexpected color. Frowning, she drove Cricket up the road's incline on the far side of the bridge and stopped to squint against the rivulets of rain in the thin window of her door.

She searched again for the bright blue spot. A bucket, caught on a branch? A piece of tarp? A thin piece of the blue lifted, as if waving. Her heart pounding, Emma slid the door open a crack for a better look. Cilla had been wearing bright blue. Surely it wasn't…

Emma gasped as the branch broke and the blue, definitely a small figure, whirled in the churning water. Slamming the sliding door open, Emma lunged from the buggy to race along the creek's bank. In her peripheral vision, she saw Cricket trot on to her lane and head toward the barn.

"Cilla! Can you get toward the bank?" She held her breath when the girl grabbed on to a partially submerged shrub. The shrub stretched. Emma sucked in a breath when it held. Too far though. It was still too far from the bank. She couldn't reach her. If she tried, they'd both be in the roiling water. Her eyes darted between the patch of blue in the creek to the ground between her and the girl. No branches down. Nothing she could reach or break. And no time to do so.

Cilla's face, what she could see of it from the hair hanging like ropes about her, was white. Her *kapp* was gone. The girl opened her mouth but Emma couldn't hear anything over the roar of the water. Even as she watched, Cilla was pulled farther along the shrub's slender branches, stripping leaves down its length as she clung to its precarious safety.

Emma glanced from her to the bridge. Between them, there were no more snags to grab, no more branches to reach, only angry water before the lethal culverts. Heart hammering,

Emma lifted her skirt out of the way and ran. Her feet were slapping on the concrete when passing debris bumped Cilla and the shrub was torn from her hands. She was again in the grip of the turbulent flood.

Emma skidded to a halt at the bridge's center as the girl bobbed toward her.

"Can you get to the edge? Try to move out of the current!" Pressing her hands to her mouth, Emma watched as the girl valiantly struggled to evade the current's strong grip.

"Cilla!" Emma screamed when the bright blue disappeared. Her own breath was bursting by the time it popped back to the surface.

The creek curved at the bridge, leaving the water to flow along its side before racing into the culverts at the end. As Cilla careened toward her in the muddy waters, Emma dropped to her belly onto the cold, wet concrete. The rough surface abraded her elbows as she edged forward. Menacing water rushed beneath her shoulders and chest as she inched out as far as she dared without plunging into the deluge. Sputtering at the splashing against her face, she focused on the converging bright blue. She had one chance to grab Cilla before the girl was washed through the twenty-foot culvert. A trip she might not complete or survive.

Please *Gott*, let one chance be enough.

Chapter Eighteen

Cilla's eyes were wide. She was alternating between gasping for air and pressing her lips tight against the roiling water that splashed into her face. Her desperate paddling had no effect.

"No!" Emma screamed. The turbulent flood swung the girl back into the teeth of the current, heading straight for the gyrating debris at the culvert. With a desperate lunge, Emma grabbed for her.

Her scrabbling hand brushed down Cilla's sodden skirt and reaching arm before she was able to clamp it around the girl's slender wrist. She grimaced in pain as the resulting jolt on her own shoulder and wrist almost pulled her into the water. Gritting her teeth, she splayed her legs to secure her position. With both hands on her precious cargo, she squirmed backward until the rough concrete was under her chest.

Cilla was on her back, bobbing along the edge of the bridge. Her white face and blue-tinged lips were barely above the surface of the splashing water. Under Emma's grip, her fragile wrist was ice-cold.

"I won't let go." Emma answered the question in the girl's frantic eyes. Cilla reached a hand free of the water to clasp one of Emma's wrists. Burying her teeth in her bottom lip, Emma focused on her grip. *Please* Gott, *give these hands strength. Please let me hang on as long as necessary.*

Emma gasped when a frigid wave lapped over the top of the concrete, soaking her dress. The creek was rising. If she didn't get Cilla to safety soon, they could both be swept away. She struggled to settle her breathing. The rising water should also help in lifting the girl. Emma just had to get her onto the bridge and then to higher ground before it got too deep.

A flash of movement upstream caught her attention. Barreling toward them in the churning water was a log about the size of the girl she was holding on to. Emma's heart leaped to her throat. If it careened into Cilla, trapping her against the concrete…

Thrusting herself backward, Emma struggled to lift the girl onto the bridge to no avail. With a frantic eye on the approaching log, she again laid prone on the concrete. Cilla's despairing sob cut through her as Emma tugged to loosen her hand. Even so, Emma jerked it free, extending it as far as she could beyond where the girl's small frame was pressed against the bridge. Bracing herself for the collision with the log, she lifted a silent prayer.

Please Gott, *please* Gott, *please* Gott.

Just before impact, the current swept the log to the side. Instead of slamming straight into Cilla, its broadside bumped against Emma's outstretched hand before it lurched on toward the culvert. Emma bit into her lip until she tasted copper when pain exploded in her wrist.

The initial splash over the concrete was now a constant flow. Emma lifted her chin to keep it above the rippling surface. Wincing, she grabbed a handful of Cilla's sodden skirt with her free hand and again tried to roll the girl onto the bridge.

"Ah! My foot! It's stuck!"

One of the girl's feet bobbed along the surface, but the other had disappeared into the muddy water at the culvert's voracious mouth. Emma stared at the churning water endeavoring to consume the log now wedged there. If she let go of Cilla's wrist to wrest her foot free, there was no guarantee she'd get her back. She couldn't risk it.

Water splashed at her shoulders. Cilla cringed, her leg disappearing at a steeper angle as the flood lifted her body while anchoring her foot. Letting go of the skirt, Emma shifted her hand to cradle Cilla's head above the water. Her fierce gaze bore into the girl's frightened eyes.

"I'm not going anywhere."

Cilla dipped her chin in a tiny nod, though it was hard to tell as the girl's teeth were chattering so forcefully.

Water raced over the backs of Emma's legs. She began to shiver. Her arms were cramping. Her hands, the parts that weren't already numb with cold, ached. *Just please let them stay secure!* Cilla didn't need to know her fears. She pushed up a smile.

"Guess I won't be needing a bath tonight. I'm getting one here."

Emma squeezed her eyes shut to quell threatening tears, then shook her head at her own foolishness. How could anyone tell she was crying with all the water in her face, and what difference did it make? What difference did anything make at the moment, except whether she could rescue this girl she treasured? She didn't even know if Cilla could hear her over the roar of the water, but she kept talking, hoping it would help keep at least one of them calm.

"And maybe I needed a dunking to cool off, I was that upset. But you know what? As upset as I was, or maybe still am, I still love your grandfather. Does that surprise you? Ah, I can see that it doesn't. You're right in what you've said before. He's not bad for a grandpa. And I know he'll make a good husband. He was a wonderful one to your *grossmammi*. He doesn't get everything right. But he tries. And he feels deeply. And if he makes a mistake— which he did today, didn't he—I know he'll try not to do it again. Besides, as *Gott* directs us to do, we need to forgive, as I hope your grandpa will forgive me when I make mistakes in the future, which, for sure and certain, I will."

If I get a chance to do so.

"So, when we get out of this mess, I suppose I need to tell the foolish man that I'll marry him if he'll still have me. Besides, I can't wait to be in a family that includes you. Does that suit you?"

Cilla's face contorted. Her head, cradled in Emma's numb hand, jerked in a nod. Emma took a few ragged breaths herself. The water on the bridge was over her thighs. She couldn't feel the hand that wrapped around Cilla's slender wrist. The girl's lips were tinged with blue. Her hips now disappeared into the roiling water. More debris was tumbling downstream. If it hit them, not only could it hurt Cilla, but it could sweep Emma off the bridge and into the turbulent water on the other side. Although she wanted to close her eyes, she kept them focused on Cilla's and her trembling lips tipped in a smile.

Thomas, I'm sorry. I'm sorry I was too proud to have you when I had the chance. I'm sorry I was worrying about being secondhand when our Savior was born in a manger, not even a house or a bed. I'm sorry I won't have a chance to be your wife, who I know you will cherish, whatever you call me, because that is who you are. I'm sorry...

Thomas wearily pushed up from his hunched perch on the chair's armrest. Nothing would be solved by staring at the wall. And he had work to do. Dropping the towels into his chair, he headed for the door. He'd lived without Emma as a wife and partner for four years; he could continue to do so, although there was no joy in the prospect. And he wouldn't be alone; regardless of Emma's decision, Cilla was staying with him. His son would just have to understand.

While crossing the porch, he halted at the sight of the black-and-white kitten curled up on a metal chair. It sleepily lifted its head under his stare. He'd expected Cilla to take comfort in the creature. If the cat was here, where was Cilla? The calf was in the barn, but it was too rambunctious to stay still long enough for someone to cry… Or had she said…try?

Oh, no. Had Cilla gone after Emma to try to rectify his mistake? His jaw tightened. *Ja*, it would be something the girl would do. Run was synonymous with upset in her definition. How far could she have gotten in this rain? And Emma! He'd been so thrilled when she'd arrived, he hadn't thought about how she'd made it across the creek. Surely, even upset, she wouldn't try to cross it when flooded?

He headed for the barn at a jog. A short while later, a reluctant Banner left the barn at a brisk trot. Thomas peered through the rivulets on the glass, straining to see any sign of Cilla along the road. *Please don't let her have tried the rock crossing.* But as the distance passed, there was no sign of her.

Although the rain slowed to a stop by the time he'd reached the bridge, Thomas didn't need to see out to know it was underwater. He could tell by Banner's fidgeting and hesitation. Thomas leaned out the buggy door to review the torrent. Dropping the lines, he hurtled from the rig. Heart in mouth, he raced toward the two figures in the water.

Water splashed about his legs as he bounded onto the bridge to grasp Emma's shoulder. Jerking at his touch, she looked up at him, her eyes wide with wonder in her white face.

"I got her."

Emma stammered with cold. "Her f-foot is s-stuck."

Thomas nodded. Lying down beside her, he hissed in a breath at the frigid water that immediately soaked him. He reached out to squeeze Cilla's frighteningly cold hand before working his hands down her leg to her unseen foot. Tangled debris, battling to get through the culverts, surged about his arms. He grimaced as a whirling bough gouged his chilled hand.

He was working blind, one hand gripping Cilla's slender foot, the other tracing the branches and sticks that entrapped her. Beside him, over the roar of the water, he could hear Emma and Cilla coughing against the rampant spray. The sound added strength to his powerful blacksmith hands as he snapped wet branches and shoved aside sodden leaves being sucked into the vacuum of the culvert. With a prayer and a final tug, he pulled her foot free. Cilla's leg bobbed to the surface, and her body swung with the water flowing over the bridge.

Scooping her up with one arm, Thomas

grabbed Emma's elbow with the other hand and hauled her to her feet. Sloughing through the rushing water, he guided her up the ascent a few feet above the flooded creek before sagging with his precious cargo onto the wet blacktop. He pulled them into his embrace and buried his face against Emma's neck.

"I was so afraid I'd lose you both."

Afraid to hug their shivering forms too tightly in case of injuries, he settled for the assurance of their rapid breathing and their pounding hearts pressed to his. They were alive. Raising his head, he peered at their pale faces. Emma's eyes brimmed with tears as they met his. Cilla's were closed, her head leaning against his shoulder.

"Cilla, Cilla, are you all right?" Hypothermia was a threat. Along with other injuries incurred in the turbulent water. Her eyes didn't open, although she mumbled.

"What?" Thomas bent his head closer.

"She said she loved you." The words were still whisper thin, but Thomas, his eyes rounding, heard them.

"And that she'll marry you." The girl's eyes drifted open.

He shifted as if to rise. "You're shaking with cold. I need to get you into the buggy."

"Not until she agrees to be part of our family."

Thomas's lips tilted to match those of the girl he cradled. "Stubborn."

"I take after my *grossdaddi*."

His gaze locked with Emma's. "I've apologized enough to you that I should be well practiced. I…" His throat bobbed in a hard swallow. "I always associated joy with Priscilla. Something I haven't felt since she was gone. Until you. I just didn't know how to acknowledge it or say it again. But I do now. Emma, you're the one that makes my heart overflow with joy."

Her eyes were luminous. "You never said my name before."

"Truly?" He was disturbed at the thought.

"Truly. I would've noticed."

"Emma. My dear Emma." He kissed her brow. "I'll make up for it now." Tenderly, he settled his treasures more closely into the protection of his embrace. "Now, please say yes, so I can marry you and keep you by my side. And so when my granddaughter wants to see you, she doesn't have to cross the creek to do it."

Cilla grinned at his words. To his vast relief, color was returning to her face.

And under his warm regard, to Emma's as well. "Oh, Thomas. You have such a way with words."

His voice was solemn, as was his gaze. "I

know what love is. I loved Priscilla. She was a wonderful woman and wife. The bride of my youth, the mother of my children. I couldn't have asked for better. But I couldn't ask for a better woman than you to grow old with. Please share with me the rest of your years. And allow me to treasure you for the rest of mine. I love you, Emma."

This time, her "Oh, Thomas" was breathless. And his kiss ensured it remained so.

Epilogue

Emma glanced out the open window at the clattering of hooves on the lane. Her heart leaped at the sight of Thomas descending from his buggy. She looked down just in time to stop the treadle wheel with her hand.

"Don't run the needle over your finger like I did when I was learning."

Cilla looked up from her concentration on the apricot fabric under the presser foot, a wide smile on her face. "I can't believe I'm making a quilt."

Emma rested her hand on the girl's shoulder. "Thomas and I have many warm memories of your *grossmammi*. We thought she'd appreciate that her dresses would help make a quilt to warm you."

Speaking of warmth, Emma patted her cheek as the door opened and Thomas stepped inside. Was she going to flush with pleasure every time he came into view? And why not? She'd waited long enough to be the one his gaze sought as soon as he entered a room. Her blush deepened as she recalled Susannah's knowing look when she'd seen them together at church the Sunday after the creek flooded. The matchmaker admitted she'd recognized that Emma knew in her heart all along the special someone she longed for. Susannah was just giving her head the opportunity to figure it out as well. And she'd had help from a miniature matchmaker in doing it.

It'd taken the past two weeks to write to the forest of suitors, telling them that while she'd appreciated their interest, she was no longer available for a relationship. Henry Troyer took her news in good stead, although he shook his head in regret. He'd shaken it more vigorously when she'd mentioned Elizabeth was still single.

Wearing his own smile, Thomas gently clasped her palm in his broad, callused one. "How are your hands feeling, Emma?"

Her wrist, from where she'd jammed it on the log, and Cilla's ankle that'd been tangled in the debris, had been swollen for a week following the creek interlude. Cilla had recovered fully, but the blow had aggravated the arthritis in Emma's wrist, along with her hands. Thomas had said he'd build her a shop at his place if she wanted. But she didn't know yet what she wanted. Besides him as her husband in two weeks' time.

"Always better entwined with yours."

Lifting their joined hands, Thomas placed a gentle kiss on every knuckle he could find exposed. The look he gave her over them was all Emma could've ever hoped for.

"I heard from Noah. He plans to make it home for the wedding. Are you sure you don't mind that he's planning to stay?"

Emma smiled. She was going from a leftover blessing to not only being blessed with a new husband and granddaughter, but a new stepson living at home as well. Thomas's youngest son had decided the bigger community was not for him and was returning to Miller's Creek. Thomas had told him of the nutcracker he'd made. Noah thought the nutcrackers, as well as some other items Thomas had in mind, would be good sellers in the tourist-popular Shipshe location. The additional work would be enough to keep both of them busy in the shop, with Emmanuel handling the products in Indiana.

Thomas had been quietly elated at the possibility. Emma was elated to be able to share his joy with him.

"I'm sure. I always enjoyed Noah when he was growing up next door. Besides, *Gott* has always advised to love thy neighbor as thyself. Just like I've always done his father."

"Love thy neighbor as thyself?" Pursing his lips, Thomas tipped his head as he considered the words. When his gaze again connected with hers, Emma's heart swelled at the adoration she saw in it. "I can say, Emma, for sure and certain, I love you more."

* * * * *

Dear Reader,

I never know when a character in a book might unexpectedly nudge me for a story of their own. Emma was such a character, from when she first appeared in *Their Unpredictable Path*. She wanted a match. I wanted to find her one. Little did I expect to discover that she'd already found the one she longed for years earlier. But, as the beau and later husband of her best friend, Thomas was forever out of reach. Until now…

The Greek language had seven different words for what we refer to in one word—love. Their language differentiated between romantic love, brotherly love, even love of a parent for a child. How wonderful that God gives us such capacity for love and loved us first and so abundantly.

Another romance is brewing in Miller's Creek. To keep updated on what might be next, stop by jocelynmcclay.com or visit me on Facebook.

May God Bless You,
Jocelyn McClay

Get 3 FREE REWARDS!

We'll send you 2 FREE Books **plus** a FREE Mystery Gift.

FREE
Value Over
$20

Both the **Love Inspired®** and **Love Inspired® Suspense** series feature compelling novels filled with inspirational romance, faith, forgiveness and hope.

YES! Please send me 2 FREE novels from the Love Inspired or Love Inspired Suspense series and my FREE gift (gift is worth about $10 retail). After receiving them, if I don't wish to receive any more books, I can return the shipping statement marked "cancel." If I don't cancel, I will receive 6 brand-new Love Inspired Larger-Print books or Love Inspired Suspense Larger-Print books every month and be billed just $6.49 each in the U.S. or $6.74 each in Canada. That is a savings of at least 16% off the cover price. It's quite a bargain! Shipping and handling is just 50¢ per book in the U.S. and $1.25 per book in Canada.* I understand that accepting the 2 free books and gift places me under no obligation to buy anything. I can always return a shipment and cancel at any time by calling the number below. The free books and gift are mine to keep no matter what I decide.

Choose one:
- ☐ **Love Inspired Larger-Print** (122/322 BPA GRPA)
- ☐ **Love Inspired Suspense Larger-Print** (107/307 BPA GRPA)
- ☐ **Or Try Both!** (122/322 & 107/307 BPA GRRP)

Name (please print)

Address   Apt. #

City   State/Province   Zip/Postal Code

Email: Please check this box ☐ if you would like to receive newsletters and promotional emails from Harlequin Enterprises ULC and its affiliates. You can unsubscribe anytime.

Mail to the Harlequin Reader Service:
IN U.S.A.: P.O. Box 1341, Buffalo, NY 14240-8531
IN CANADA: P.O. Box 603, Fort Erie, Ontario L2A 5X3

Want to try 2 free books from another series? Call 1-800-873-8635 or visit www.ReaderService.com.

---

*Terms and prices subject to change without notice. Prices do not include sales taxes, which will be charged (if applicable) based on your state or country of residence. Canadian residents will be charged applicable taxes. Offer not valid in Quebec. This offer is limited to one order per household. Books received may not be as shown. Not valid for current subscribers to the Love Inspired or Love Inspired Suspense series. All orders subject to approval. Credit or debit balances in a customer's account(s) may be offset by any other outstanding balance owed by or to the customer. Please allow 4 to 6 weeks for delivery. Offer available while quantities last.

Your Privacy—Your information is being collected by Harlequin Enterprises ULC, operating as Harlequin Reader Service. For a complete summary of the information we collect, how we use this information and to whom it is disclosed, please visit our privacy notice located at corporate.harlequin.com/privacy-notice. From time to time we may also exchange your personal information with reputable third parties. If you wish to opt out of this sharing of your personal information, please visit readerservice.com/consumerschoice or call 1-800-873-8635. **Notice to California Residents**—Under California law, you have specific rights to control and access your data. For more information on these rights and how to exercise them, visit corporate.harlequin.com/california-privacy.

LIRLIS23

HARLEQUIN
PLUS

Try the best multimedia subscription service for romance readers like you!

Read, Watch and Play.

Experience the easiest way to get the romance content you crave.

Start your **FREE TRIAL** at
<u>www.harlequinplus.com/freetrial</u>.